Pr

This book is based upon a cc individual fictional short stoı short but tantalizing enough ... ng that someone out there perhaps someone that they know or may have heard about has gone through something similar. The stories are quite racy, full of suspense, mystery, and action. Ideally this book is best suited for short journey's where you don't want to be particularly heavily engaged in a read that you cannot finish, but in the knowledge that you can finish one story quickly, and always know that that another exciting story is only a page or two away...... These stories are meant to be uplifting and just enough to get your day started with a spring in your step, and leaving you with a slight chuckle on your face.

Libraries
ReadLearnConnect

THIS BOOK IS PART OF ISLINGTON READS BOOKSWAP SCHEME

Please take this book and either return it to a Bookswap site or replace with one of your own books that you would like to share.

If you enjoy this book, why not join your local Islington Library and borrow more like it for free?

Find out about our FREE e-book, e-audio, newspaper and magazine apps, activities for pre-school children and other services we have to offer at www.islington.gov.uk/libraries

Content

Content

48 HRS

My daughter Nikki had been suffering from osteoporosis for ten years; the illness would often restrict her from many form's of school activities such as athletics P.E and other grind - boning activities she would normally be required to participate in being a young school girl, but generally speaking Nikki would do her best in coping with her disability the best way she could. Nikki would often visit her local doctor Dr Jones once a month to let him know how she was getting on. Dr Jones was a retiring doctor who always had plenty of time to sit down and discuss with her, and ask her how she was getting on, and whether or not she had found herself a boy friend, he was just like a father, he was so kind. It wasn't long before Dr Jones was due to retire and "Lemming" was about to replace him. Lemming was terrible; he never had any time for me and always rushed me out like cattle. "Lemming" was half the age of Dr Jones, and always stunk of alcohol, he seemed to be the one that really should have been seeing a doctor, not me! He was so quick to call in the next patient, this used to infuriate me madly, but I just kept it all bottled up. My illness began to get worse, and after a few months I was finding it increasingly difficult in doing the simplest of tasks, like opening a can of bake beans, it was becoming embarrassing having to depend on my father to do everything like that for me, I hated the fact that I was a bit of a burden to my dad; I was an only child living with my father, my mother had left me as a child and had re - married and did not want to know anything about me.
I remember one occasion when I phoned up "Lemming" I call him Lemming because he doesn't deserve to be called a doctor, he wasn't caring; and doctors are meant to care; anyway, I explained to him that I was in pain, and do you know what he said to me? The git told me if I stopped all of that "bonking" it would get better; that's what aggravating

it he reckoned; well I never! I was so furious because at the time I didn't even have a partner, I was so mad I just slammed down the phone in anger. The next morning I could hardly get out of bed and called my dad and asked him to phone the surgery, I felt like I was going to die; dad was so worried from hearing my agonizing screams of pain screaming aah aah. Dad finally got through to the surgery after phoning continuously for more than a hour and a half of the phone being continuously engaged, and when he did finally get through Lemming seemed so relaxed about it all, with his aloof and uncaring attitude; I only wish it was him who was suffering the pain. Anyway, I heard dad say to him after realizing just how uncaring he was being; I heard dad say to him you had better get your fat arse down here right now mate. Lemming finally arrived three hours later stinking of "scotch" and muttered a whole load of nonsense about the stupid traffic, and how he had to do a diversion because of a busted water main, then he said to me now what seems to be the problem. By the smell of him he seemed to have the problem. I really didn't want him anywhere near my daughter, but I just couldn't bare to see the pain Nikki was in, and desperately wanted him to do anything that he could to alleviate her from the agonizing pain she was suffering. By this time her face had gone completely pale. She looked awful. Lemming suggested Nikki needed a bone marrow, a bone marrow I replied!! He said yep there's no alternative, that's the best solution, but he said there is only one problem; you can't get it on the National Health. They've stopped it; you're going to have to have it done privately. Privately! I yelled, how much is that going to cost me? £6000 he replied, but I can't afford that; I'm already in arrears with my mortgage. I didn't know where to turn, and what made it worse, he insisted that it needed to be done within 48HRS. I tried to raise the money from everywhere; I went to all the high street banks, they all rejected me because I was made redundant and had county court judgments against me, and the bottom line was me having to scrape around from family and friends, which was so embarrassing because I had to get in touch with family members which I hadn't seen for years, but it had to be done. Anyway, I managed to mussel together £4000, but still needed £2000 more; there was three hours to go before Nikki's appointment for the operation. Nikki was booked in for a 3. 30pm appointment; I knew I tried my best and that I had went too all the people that I knew; and that there was no one else I could think of where I could go to raise the rest of the money. Anyway, I knew by hook or by crook I was going to get her down there, and she was going to be operated on. We arrived only to be told that the standard charge had gone up by £1000!!!!!!!!!! I was devastated, it was bad enough getting what I had, let alone finding some more. That was it for me! I jumped in a taxi straight to Westminster, told the cabby to hold on a minute, and to keep the motor running; I grabbed hold of the first MP I laid my eyes on, grabbed him around the throat, brought him down to Harley street where the surgery was, and where Nikki was waiting to be seen and told him you better sort this out now…………

TAKING ADVANTAGE

It started off with a gentle kiss. I had been working at the law firm for two months when David the boss awarded me with a kiss on the mouth for finishing off a mountain load of typing work he had plonked on my desk. Initially I was so stunned by the shear amount he had loaded on me I nearly had a heart attack; I must have gazed at it for about ten minutes before finally getting stuck in, and after about fifteen minutes of digesting my task, I knuckled down and finished it in two days, and that's only because I was quick; and I can tell you what a relief it was at that. The kiss which David landed on me took me completely by surprise as I had not been expecting it; and considering I'd only been working there for two months and hardly knew him, I felt it was somewhat inappropriate; but the irony of it was I was so keen on making a good impression I just smiled and let it ride. That kiss was to be the start of a stream of unwanted gestures and compliments about my boobs and certain parts of my anatomy which I needn't go into; he would use just about any excuse he could to squeeze past me whilst I were doing my usual photocopying, which I believe was placed in the tight corner of the room for David's cunning pleasure only so that he could rub his you know what on me, it was terrible. If it hadn't of been for the money, I would have told him to stuff his job. I thought things were a little strange when after just six months I was promoted to "Personal Assistant" with a salary increase of 10%. At the time I didn't give it much of a thought because I thought to myself it would ease me up a little on the mortgage, but that conniving little bugger had more up his sleeves than you would have known. All the while I bet he must have been thinking, if I give her a raise I'll get what I want! She'll give me some "unjumbo." Unfortunately David's plan was to backfire on him and all he ended up with was a hefty payout of £100,000 at the industrial tribunal. What had happened was, it was Christmas Eve and the company was throwing its usual Christmas party and David had pulled me over to dance with him; I had my reservations of course but being Christmas I went along with it, I didn't want him to call me a party poop. Anyway, half way through the dance I had noticed David with a hard on! Two minutes later he had his hands around my bum! I moved his hands away immediately; it was meant to have been a friendly dance; then the next thing I felt was him trying to get his tongue down my neck. It was awful….. That was it! I pushed him off and ran into the toilet sobbing, and to my horror three minutes later there he was again, like some deranged maniac from hell; he had done enough damage as it was, but , he had the temerity to follow me straight into the ladies loo, without any hesitation, none whatsoever; I thought the ladies toilets was supposed to be a no go out of bounds area for men; well some how it didn't seem to apply to David he was like some raving maniac, possessed or something. Anyway he came busting in and saw me crying, and do you know what he did; he started trying to rip my knickers off. I screamed!!!!!!! It seemed hopeless because the music was so loud; but someone did hear me, it was Shirley the main foyer receptionist, she had noticed me ran off the dance floor and had seen David follow me, and knew something was wrong; she knew what David was like because he had pestered her several times before as well. Anyway, she came in the nick of time, and saved me because that bastard surely would have raped me. Anyway, I weren't going to leave it at that; oh no! I reported him to the police, and naturally David denied it all, and told the police I was up for it, and the police let him go. I knew I couldn't go back to work, I wouldn't have been able to face him at work, however, I never imagined the bastard would have had the cheek to sack me. It was three days into the New Year and I received a letter in the post saying that I had been sacked for being incompetent, incompetent… well, I wasn't having any of it, and took the matter to the Industrial Tribunal, and

David was found guilty of improper behaviour towards me, and charged with unfair dismissal; I had Shirley at the hearing and she confirmed that David had pestered her too; they awarded me £100,000. David looked stunned at the amount he had to pay me; his jaw dropped, and as I was making my way out of the courtroom, I looked over at David, as I could feel his eyes staring at me; and noticed him clench his teeth in anger, he was absolutely gutted.

AFFAIR

We had been married for fifteen years and had three children Kate, Peter and Sarah who were all under fifteen. Sex had been pretty good between the both of us; we went out for meals once a month, and to my understanding things were all right. I was wrong; Stanley had not been satisfied for a long time, and what he was doing all the time by taking me out once a month was simply nursing the bruise rather than addressing the problem and trying to solve it, he simply brushed it under the carpet, and hoped it would go away, but the problem would always be there; if we had simply addressed the problem perhaps we could have got to the route of the problem and tried to solve it. But no, he simply brushed the matter under the carpet and went off and did his own thing and pretended the matter did not exist. It felt like we were living two separate lives. Anyway, I suspected something was up when Stanley came home with a ripped vest, a love bite on his neck and scratches all over his body; I noticed this as he made his way through to the bathroom; how did you do that Stanley I asked? Oh I caught it on a nail in the garage; Stanley's response seemed quite nervy!!!!! Oh, Stanley how did you get that bruise on your neck? I questioned him again, referring to the love bite which was so clear to see (Stanley) oh!! I scraped it on the exhaust pipe he replied. A few weeks went by and Stanley kept finding just about every excuse under the sun for going out. He wasn't really the going out type, he never used to go out before; he was always bogged down totally engaged in stripping down his prized possession, his ford Capri, and putting it back together again, he got a lot of pleasure out of doing that; much more it would appear than he got out of me; he spent all his blooming time in that garage. I knew something wasn't quite right and I only wish Stanley could have been able to talk to me about it. When one day I just had enough, he wasn't paying any attention to me, he couldn't even be bothered to give me a hug as he normally did, so I decided I'd confront him about it, I wanted to get to the crutz of the matter and made a decision to find out exactly where Stanley was getting his excitement from. I was curious to know what was so fascinating so consuming that Stanley wouldn't even spend any quality time with me, I wanted this from him like crazy, I needed him to show me affection, I felt like it can't go on like this, because sooner or later it would get to a stage where I would say to Stanley its me or the garage Stanley; so what I did I hired a "Private Detective" to follow his every move. And for weeks John the Private Detective could not find anything suspicious, but he did notice something peculiar; there was one particular place Stanley would go every day and spend two to three hours completely alone, it was with this damn horse in a field about a mile from our house. He secretly had bought this beast and kept it secret from me. Why didn't he just tell me?

A LESSON

This is a story about a school of excellence which was put into place to teach discipline; law and order to young men, and show them how to behave properly and how to have respect and acquire the right morals and principals which sadly is something missing in today's society. Colvin's, the school of excellence seemed to have the correct impact on the men and was recognized as a place where young men really did seem to improve as law abiding citizens. But as with everything, there exist a group of people who no matter what privileges they already have, they are not content with having respect for people's properties, or for that matter, no respect for people in general; and they certainly have no desire of wanting to work for their living. They believe, if I can get something for nothing, I'll sure as hell take the chances and get it. The school I suppose can be described as a type of army training centre where there's some real tough nut soldiers on twenty four-hour patrol, always alert and ready to wring someone's neck, or to kick the hell out of them if they tried to be funny; the officers always seemed so alert and ready to respond to any person brave enough, or stupid enough which ever way you like to look at it, who might chance their luck in trying to attempt to run away. Anyway, one afternoon word got out that some dope was coming in, and (Mick) was absolutely dying for a puff, and really could not resist asking one of the lads for a joint. Mick perhaps thought he could get away with it. Anyway, what had happened was one of the inmates, a friend of his kindly gave him a roll up, and Mick was ever so delighted to get his fix, and went off to the toilet to quietly sneak a much deserved puff; unknown to Mick (John Flemming) one of the senior patrol officers was on duty that evening; John came over to us as not only a law enforcer but a kind of fatherly figure. He often used to lecture us trying to explain to us the true meanings of rights and wrongs and how we should aim to be respectful members of society, and live in a socially acceptable way, and obey the law. Anyway, what had happened was he came strolling down the corridors head high up to the sky with a real proud look on his face, thinking to himself I wonder how my pupils are doing to day? He really thought we had paid attention to what he had said to us, and would be following it up by nothing other than shining examples, did we eck! The potent smell of marijuana burning was suddenly picked up by Johns highly sensitive nostrils, he instantly thought to himself those blinking good for nothing's are up to their dirty tricks again. John's nostrils led him directly towards where Mick was having his puff, in the toilet. Mick thought he was on a good one, feeling a little light headed, or I really should say out of his nut, having his much-deserved smoke, until John came along and spoilt it all. At first John just couldn't believe his eye's at what he was seeing, because he had somewhat of admiration for Mick, or at least Mick thought so; John had made it absolutely clear that anyone caught doing such a thing would not only lose time but would also endure a lengthy stay in solitary confinement, and on top of that receive "fifty lashes" to the rear. The fact that Mick had disobeyed John infuriated him intensely, because he thought we had lost respect for him; this was nonsense, we did look up to John, but were only doing the things that teenagers did at that time. Anyway, what had happened, he busted into the toilets caught me red handed, grabbed me by the scruff of my neck, I thumped him one, he thumped me back; tried to get me into a half nelson, failed miserably! Realized that I was going to be too strong for him, he pressed his panic alarm button, along came rushing to his aid three hefty mean looking colleague's of his, who seemed like they were having a bad day anyway, they held me down, face down to the ground kicked the living daylights out of me and dragged me off into a cold dark room and left me there for three weeks, only coming by twice a day to shove some food through the cat flap, yelling, grubs up, It was terrible. The three weeks I spent in there I could tell you, honestly felt like three years. Anyway I finally got out and back in the company of the rest of the lads; and I could tell you what a relief it was at that. The following day I had to attend a kind of court martial, the only difference was, I weren't allowed to go home; anyway, I was severely disciplined; but despite the original threat of loosing time, I was granted a temporary reprieve, because John had put in a good word in for me to the commanding officer, and pleaded for a more lenient sentence; despite the little bust up which I had with John in the toilets, he admired me for my achievements in the class room and especially on the football pitch, because I was a bit of a wizard!!! And also he thought I had suffered enough down the dark room and would not be foolish enough to go back down there. (Todd) one of the lads who also was sent here was beginning to get home sick, and one afternoon he called me over to a corner and said to me, I'm going to get out of this hell forsaken place, I'll crack up, it's driving me mad he said. I asked him how he was going to do it. You got armed guards up to the eyeballs, how you going to get out? Todd said to me you know when the food van comes; I'm going to hide in one of the empty containers. The following day he did just that, only to be spotted by one of the armed guards who swiftly frog-marched him back to his room. Scott was not deterred by his capture, and was determined as hell to get out; he had spoken to me several times about how he planned to do it. He waited and waited until one day he spotted his opportunity; he spotted two of the armed guards to the far end of the perimeter fence, the food van arrived as it usually did, at one o'clock sharp. The gates opened and Scott made a dash for it! Totally leaving me behind, he scarperred through the gates, I started running as well, as Scott was not the only one eager to get out; I noticed the gate starting to close, and by the skin of my teeth, I just about managed to get out, only to be spotted by one of the guards who fired a shot at me. I heard the bullet go whizzing passed my ear; by this time Scott had disappeared through the thick forest; I couldn't see him amongst all the thick bushes; he had disappeared. The guards had got their dogs out and were perusing us with vengeance, when I heard one of them say, let him go Bill; which he did, and before I knew it, I could feel this extremely agitated "Doberman Pinscher" biting at my arm. Bill had caught up with me and was trying to restrain his dog, which seemed to mistake me for his tea! Anyway, I was escorted back and unknown to me, Scott had been chased down in the same fashion with the dogs, and was captured and brought back. On my arrival to the training ground, and who do you think was at the gate; none other than "Captain John Flemming" who had a look on his face of utter disgust. As I made my way to the courtroom to be disciplined once again, there to my amazement were three other opportunists who thought they too would take their chances; there was Simon Alexander - Anthony Melvin & Sidney Joyce. As we walked along the corridor leading to the courtroom, there was something rather peculiar I had noticed; there were £1 coins deliberately and strategically placed conspicuously all over parts of the corridor. I thought to myself this is a little odd? Simon had noticed it too; they had been deliberately left there by John Flemming to tempt any willing person to pocket it knowing full well that they would be caught on camera. Anyway, surprisingly enough nobody was foolish enough to take it, and as I entered into the court room, sitting down, was Simon, who whispered to me, did you see those £1 coins scattered all over the place? I replied, Yeah. He replied; it's a set up.

Hayley, my sister grew an instant dislike to me when mother bought me a doll for my fifth birthday. That day, Hayley was sent to bed early for repeatedly putting her finger in the plug hole. In a rage, she cut the hair off my brand new doll, reducing me at the time to tears, and I've never forgiven her for that. I don't know why she hated me so much; perhaps it was because I was born, or simply the fact that I was breathing; perhaps it may have been the fact that I had all the attention for a whole two years before she was born, I just don't know. When Hayley found out that I knew what she had done to my doll, and that I had told mother what she had done, she came after me in such a rage; furious that I had spilled the beans on her, she came at me with her razor sharp fingernails, which she refused to have cut. She wouldn't have her fingernails cut because at the time I guess she must have truly believed mother was actually trying to cut her fingers off; ooh, she was so naughty. Anyway, Hayley came rushing towards me, and took one hell of a swipe at my face with her razor sharp fingernails; god knows what damage she would have done if she had caught me; anyway, I narrowly escaped by dodging out of her way missing me by inches. Mother heard her raging tantrum and shouted out Hayley!!!! Go to your room now. Hayley made her way up the stairs and towards her bedroom in buckets full of tears, crying out hysterically. That afternoon Hayley heard me having such a fun time playing with Linda our next door neighbour in the garden. I looked up at the window, and noticed how miserably she looked, she had a look of envy on her face, wishing she could be out here too; but all she could do was to watch on painfully. It was time for tea, and as a punishment, Hayley wasn't allowed to have her tea with the rest of the family; she was still on punishment and had to have her tea in her bedroom. I on the other hand sat comfortably in front of the television having my tea and watching play school. After all, she had brought it upon herself. The evening was coming to an end; the time was around seven o'clock, and time for me to go to bed. I thought Hayley was sleeping, and sneaked into our bedroom tentatively and slid soundlessly on the bottom layer of our bunk-bed, and just as I was about to get my head under the covers, out sprang Hayley from the top layer of the bed, like a blooming maniac, with her razor sharp claw like fingernails; she came at me with a vengeance, she suddenly pounced on me scratching my face, I screamed!!! Mum!!!!!!! Hayley scratched me, look; pointing towards the two-inch scratch Hayley had inflicted on the left side of my face; mother was furious and with her slipper she gave Hayley the hiding of her life, she cried all night. Mother separated us for two weeks; but I guess after about two weeks of separation, Hayley started to miss me; she eventually started to speak to me, and started to act a little kinder towards me. I slowly began to build a little trust in Hayley. I actually think it probably had something to do with dad giving her a thorough reprimand which made the impact on her. I began to notice slight changes in Hayley's behaviour, and noticed how she was becoming friendlier and more appreciating towards me, so I allowed her to play with my toys.

MY BABY

It was such a wonderful summer's day, the sun was shining and I had just finished speaking to my auntie Mary in America. I had been planning on visiting her in the New-Year. Phoebe my baby was looking a bit restless so I decided to take her out for a walk, so we headed for the park, and on my way back from the park I thought to myself I might as well do a little bit of shopping and headed for my local supermarket. When we got there, you know how it is; you always end up realizing that you need more than what you originally bargained for. Anyway, when we got there, I decided rather than trolleying Phoebe around with me, I might as well leave her in the crèche area to play with the rest of the toddlers whilst I quickly do my bit, then return to her once I had finished. The shop floor had been rearranged and the nappies weren't in their usual place and I could not find them for the life of me, so I approached one of the staff stacking the shelves and he directed me to where the nappies had been relocated. I thought I had just about everything I needed and decided to treat phoebe and myself to a box of chocolates. I got the box of chocolates and was making my way to the cashier. There were only two people in the queue at the time and I thought to myself brilliant! Because I hate it when you have to wait a long time to be served, then bang! I remembered I'd forgotten the milk, and dashed back as quickly as I could so I would not miss out too much in the queue, but have and behold, the milk had been relocated as well, and after walking up and down the isle several times looking scantically disorientated, I found it; and quickly dashed back to the cashiers in hope that when I got back to the queue it would still be relatively empty. When I got there the queue had built up several folds; I was so mad!! Anyway, I finally got served, after waiting, which seemed to be forever, and was making my way back to the crèche area where I left Phoebe. At first I couldn't see her amongst the twenty to twenty five kids that were playing there. Phoebe? I soon realized that Phoebe wasn't together with the rest of kids at all, and anyway I would have been able to recognize her almost instantly with her distinctive bright pink jacket. Phoebe! I screamed in my head!!!!!!!!!!!! Oh my god, oh my god, I dropped my shopping bags and started screaming hysterically!!!! Phoebe! Phoebe! And started rushing around the crèche area asking everyone have you seen this little girl with a bright pink jacket on, she's around two years of age. No; everyone replied. I rushed back to the store and saw a security guard; he then notified all the guards to be on alert and told them to be on the look out for her. I rushed out to the car park to see if she had made her way out there, and to my horror I noticed this young girl walking off with her, I screamed stop!!! The girl turned around realizing that I was her mother and she ran off, leaving Phoebe confused and crying. It was terrible. It was terrible…………

BAD BUY

I had just started my new job, and thought to myself, I'll treat myself to a car. I really didn't know much about cars, so I got my sisters' boyfriend Michael to get one for me. He seemed to know quite a bit about cars; he bought a new one every year, so naturally I assumed he would be the best person to get one for me. I didn't have an awful lot to spend; in fact I only had £500 so I gave the "monkey" to Michael and left it to his own devises to come up with something half-decent. What I hadn't realized was, that, that scheming little boyfriend of my sisters' Michael, had a bad gambling habit, and what he did was, rather than doing what I specifically told him to do, and get me a decent motor, the sod only went out and bought two knackered old motors, which looked all right from the outside, but the cars was literally falling to pieces, and really on its last legs; to put it plainly, it was a complete rust box, and somewhat of a death trap. He paid £150.00 for each of them, and was trying to sell them, pocketing £200.00 for his self; he sold one straight away, for £350.00, and had someone lined up to sell the other for the same price, netting him a total profit of £200.00, but that wasn't the deal. I specifically gave Michael my £500 quid to buy one motor car, and not two. I had a hunch that Michael was hiding something from me, by the way he would stutter when I asked him haven't you found one yet? His reply was always, I'll get one soon; three months had past; surely he should have been able to get one by now. The date was approaching my 21st birthday, and I was getting extremely agitated with Michael's aloofness, so I confronted my sister Janet to find out what the devil was happening with my money which I gave to her stupid boyfriend. I was shocked to get a reply from Janet, when she responded to me saying, don't bloody ask me what Michael's doing with your money, your business with Michael, has nothing to do with me she replied. Apparently the both of them had been going through a bit of a patch; but she was my sister and the very least I expected from her, was to tell me the truth. Anyway, what had happened was, my patients had worn thin, and I went on the hunt for that elusive boyfriend of hers, only to find him, as I was walking down the high street on my way to his house; something made me look in the betting shop window; because from the back, this guy bared a splitting resemblance to Michael. Anyway, I took a closer look, and to my horror, it was him!!!!!!!!!! I stormed in, and haled out a stream of abuse at him; I had one hell of a blaze up with him; embarrassing him somewhat, with everyone looking on perplexed, and bemused. He was so embarrassed by the way I humiliated him in front of all his mates like that; he promised me that I would have either the money or the car by the end of the week. He did keep his promise I hastened to add by the threat I laid upon him with the police. Anyway, the irony was, that the git only turned up with this car which had no M.O.T, and to put it mildly was a bit of a jalopy. I was so furious; when I went to start the car up the following morning, only to find out that the bloody thing wouldn't start, so I called the AA. I was running late as it was for work; and what made it worse the AA arrived an hour later than previously arranged; and when he finally arrived, he took one look under the bonnet, and shook his head, naming with a list of things that was wrong with it; my jaw just dropped, he said to me, in short madam; it's a wreck. I thought to myself, you bastard Michael; how could you do this to me. That evening, I called Michael's house, and told him what a F..............Bastard he was to do such a thing like that to me; he tried to deny it at first, claiming, believe it or not, that the AA don't know what they're talking about; just change the battery he said. I did what he said foolishly enough, and change the battery, only to find out that the car drove like chitty chitty bang bang; the exhaust pipe firing off every five seconds, I was so annoyed. I insisted on Michael to give me all my money back, his reply to me was, well you know you get what you pay, and with that said, he slammed the phone down on me, I was so angry.

I TRIED MY BEST

This is a story about a poverish boy aged 15 who decided the only way he was going to get out of the Ghetto was to become a boxer. He was not a particularly bright boy and was never going to become a rocket scientist or get straight A's at school. Realizing this would later prove to have a psychological affect on Tommy's behaviour. But what was more worrying; he found it increasingly difficult in concentrating and studying at school. This often led Tommy into truancy and into regular fights. At the age of 18 Tommy joined Fighters Boxing Club; and at 20 Tommy turned professional. Tommy was an average fighter not particularly skilful, but fiercely intimidating with his huge frame and bulging muscles, and his height, he was six foot five, and very intimidating. Tommy's main downfall was that he always came off the worse when he fought; he was so clumsy. His fights were very scrappy; he seldom came away without cuts or bruises to his face; after his fights he would often have to be stitched up which left with huge scars on his face; he looked terrible. Tommy thought hard and was always thinking about how he would hit the big time and command huge salaries and retire early from fighting and be able to support his family and live in a huge house. I only wished that Tommy had just gone and done any old job; even if he swept the roads, cleaned offices; anything other than coming home with those huge scars on his face; it was unbearable. Tommy came home with a new scar every time he had a fight; it was becoming increasingly difficult to even recognize him at times; but all Tommy would say was that I'm going to make it bruv; don't worry, I'm going to make it. Tommy's was to have his last fight; I knew he shouldn't have fought this guy they called "Ivan the Terrible" he was massive, he had fists like basketballs, and by the footage of what I saw him do to one of his previous opponents, I knew he would do the same, or even worse to Tommy. This guy never seemed to be content with just a win on points, he always seemed as though he would have preferred to knock the head clean off his opponents and have it rolling around the ring like a football. Anyway, the fight started, and by the third round, Tommy face was covered in blood! It was terrible. I suppose a better way of describing him would be "John Merrick" Elephant Man; I think that would be a better description; and by the eighth round, the fight had to be stopped because Tommy had been knocked over too many times; but Tommy still wanted to fight on. Tommy was not a quitter, and was disgusted by the referee's decision to end the fight. Minutes later Tommy had collapsed. The doctor jumped into the ring, desperately trying to revive Tommy; they revived him and Tommy came around; but the damage had already been done. He had received permanent brain damage; it was to be Tommy's last fight; the injury Tommy received crippled him for life.

And three of them came in one after the other; it was unbelievable, I could hardly wait to hand my tickets in, and collect the cash. I won £18,000, Six Thousand Pound on each horse. Everything was going great; I decided to bank £10,000 and invest the other eight on another race. This time I decided I'd go £5,000, on take the pillow, and three grand on it's a monkey; take the pillow came first, and it's a monkey came third, so I just about broke even. I thought to myself its just a one off, so what the hell, the Grand National only comes around once a year, so I might as well av a go. What I hadn't realized was this would be the beginning of vicious addiction; I often found myself spending my last few pounds on a horse, when frankly the money could have been spent more carefully on other things. Sometimes I would go without food, cigarettes, and booze, all of which June my wife was absolutely incensed by; and would often refuse to supply me with any more money unless I jacked in the gambling. She would often say you want food - cigs and booze; stop gambling. I stopped for a couple of weeks, but only to find out whenever I turned the television on the only thing I was interested in was the races; it didn't seem as an addiction at the time. Until one day we found ourselves behind with the mortgage repayments and also with the HP which we had taken out on our new three piece suite; we had fallen into arrears; things couldn't have been more poignant when numerous red letters came flooding through the letter box, all of which I ignored, I just binned the lot; completely refusing to acknowledge it, it was almost as though they didn't non exist. June and I argued constantly; I hated it, because I knew it was my fault; but the way I viewed it, was, all I was trying to do, was to hit the big winner, and secure our family's financial situation. Albeit in the wrong way, but at the time, I really couldn't think of anything else that could have sorted us out. June seemed content working down at the launderette, earning £250.00 a week, and working all the hours of the day, but that was hardly going to give us a champagne lifestyle was it? All I wanted to was to put an end to all of that, but would she understand, oh no; you stupid woman I thought. It was I, I was the one who was at fault, she was doing the correct thing by going to work, and I, and I was the one who was out of work and just hoping to make it big. I realized it too late, when one afternoon I walked through the door only to stumble over yet another bombardment of countless red letters from the furniture, gas, electric company, you name it, I had it. Something made me looked out of the window, when I heard a car pull up outside my door, only to realize to my horror, that three mean and hefty looking body building geezers leapt out of their car and was making their way over to my door. They knocked on my door, brow!!!!!!!brow!!!!!!!!!!! Mr. Thomas! Where here to repossess the leather suite you purchased from us; and with that said, they just barged passed me making their way through the hall and lifted the single sofa's up single-handedly, I was terrified stiff!!!!!! They looked so intimidating; they took the three seater out last; whilst the meanest one out of them watched on with intent; I thought they were finished, when to my horror, they made their way up to the bedroom, and took our bed as well, I cried to them….. You can't take my bed……

BIG MISTAKE

I recently met this girl called Sue down the pub. The first time I met Sue I noticed how much of a flirt she was; I noticed how she would be flirting around with the entire guy's in the pub, she would allow them to buy her drinks. There was also something else I noticed, it was that the men who would normally be chatting her up were almost twice her age, so I thought to myself perhaps if I chatted her up, she'll fancy me more. The way we met was a little ironic because Sue had entered the pool competition; I loved to play pool; and before long it was my turn to play Sue. Sue had just beaten this old man who entered the competition and was feeling pretty confident with her victory; and she seemed to fancy herself favorably against me. The old man she beat was useless, and I guess Sue perhaps thought I was probably useless as well, and she would give me a pasting too. Anyway, by the time I set the balls up it was Sue's turn to break, because the winner of the previous game always breaks. The game was quite interesting and Sue was playing really well; considering she was a woman. She had a real determined look on her face; and really was playing to win. We cleared just about all the balls and there was one ball left on the table, the black, it was my shot and I potted it. Sue made a comment saying that I was a jammy bugger. From that moment on, we got chatting, and I offered to buy her a drink, which she accepted. Later that evening Sue asked me if I would walk her home. I said, certainly Sue, I'll just get my jacket, I got my jacket and walked her to her house which was about a mile and a half away from where the pub was; I kept on saying to her, how far is it to go? Each time she replied not too far now….. I was beginning to think she was taking me on some kind of wild goose chase or something. Anyway, we finally arrived at her house and Sue offered me a cup of coffee, and one thing led to another. Two weeks later and I began to feel a bit itchy down there; it felt like somewhat of a burning sensation that had come over me. To be honest it felt as though someone played some sort of absurd trick on me and put a vindaloo hot curry or a red-hot chilli powder down my pants. Anyway, what had happened was the feeling became so uncomfortable and unbearable I decided to visit my doctor to see what it was all about; I told him what the problem was, and he referred me to the special clinic; at this stage I was beginning to get rather worried. Anyway, I went down to the special clinic, and would you believe it, I stumbled across three old school mates, all twiddling their fingers, worried sick about what bad news the doctor would have to say to them; I watched them all sat down with a look of deep concern on their faces; they all looked embarrassed that there was someone they knew would have to be down there. Anyway, after waiting for a whole two long hours, it was my turn to be seen. I got up like a shot when they called my name, and made my way to room number 2. This way the female doctor said to me, leading me in the direction to her room; I thought to myself female doctor? What in heavens name next. Anyway, within minutes of her asking me a few questions, she promptly asked me to drop my trousers, which I did, in the most embarrassing way, thinking all the time of how my body would react. I was rather hoping that my privates would have remain in a southernly position, things couldn't have been more embarrassing, I suddenly shot up like a shot, realizing, oh my god, I'm in an embarrassing northerly position. I was so embarrassed. Anyway, after having been gently examined by this female doctor, which I might say seemed to go on forever; I was sent back to the waiting room where I had to wait for a further fifteen minutes, whilst my urine was being diagnosed, the wait was so nerve racking; and when the diagnosis was done, she called me back in and sat me down, shook her head and said "gonorrhoea" dear, I was devastated, I wanted to kill Sue. On my departure from the clinic there was only one of my ex schoolmates left waiting in the waiting room, he was still waiting to be seen, he asked me is everything all right then? I felt like saying what do you bloody think; instead I replied rather hesitantly yeah…. just in for a check up that's all. I felt like kicking myself. As soon as I got out of the clinic, I sprinted all the way to Sue's house. There was only one thing I had on my mind, I wanted to wring Sue's bloody neck, and I wanted to kill her. Anyway, I got down to Sue's, she wasn't in, so I sprinted down to the pub, heaven knows where I got the energy from, but I just couldn't wait to get hold of her and wring her neck. I got down there, and there she was talking to some guy, so I went up to her, and before she had a chance to say hi Derek, I grabbed her by the throat and dragged her outside; the guy she was talking to was wondering what the hell was going on here, the barman came rushing to her aid, trying to drag me off of her, he finally got me off of her, but not before I had busted her lips.

IS THAT YOURS

It all started when "speedy" turned up at my house one Saturday night with a brand new BMW. Is that yours speedy? Dave was his real name but we nicked name him speedy because he was a hell of a runner, so we thought we ought give him a nick-name, and from that moment on speedy was born and it stuck with him ever since. Anyway, he turned up in this spanking brand new red BMW and offered me to come out for a spin with him. I asked him where he had got it from, and he said to me his dad had just bought it and had gone on holiday for a week and left him with the keys. I didn't know whether to believe him or not, but having being so impressed with the car, I walked around it completely fascinated by it. The temptation far outweighed the risk, and all I really wanted to see was just how fast it could go. And the smell; the smell of the brand new leather interior, just put me on an instant high. Anyway, I jumped in, and speedy took off with this incredibly long wheel spin, it was wicked!!!!!

Half way down the main road, speedy spotted this old clapped out BMW with four guys around the same age as us, they looked as though they were having a night out on the town. Anyway we both ended up stopping at the red lights together, and I could sense instinctively just what was going through speedy's head, he wanted to leave those guy's for dead; it also seemed as though the guy's in the clapped out BMW wanted to leave us standing. Anyway we both stopped at the lights waiting for them to change, and by the time the lights had changed to yellow, speedy had took off like a rocket!!!!! He was like a thunderbolt, he left the clapped out BMW standing; it was so funny!! A mile down the road and speedy spotted a brand new BMW, and believe it or not, speedy wanted to burn him up as well! The race was on almost instantly! I guess we must have been doing around 90 when a police car spotted us!! This time the chase was on us! I was terrified. I told speedy stop!

Speedy paid no attention to me; he had only one thing on his mind, and that was to get away. Der der der der der der der der the sirens sounded, speedy stop! I yelled; I guess what I had to say to speedy went through one ear, and out of the other. Speedy took a sharp turn around the corner hoping to loose them, but it was no use they were still on our trail. Then suddenly, a thought came to my attention, why won't he stop; he must of have been telling me pork pies about his dad lending him the keys, it wasn't true at all. After about ten miles of shear hell of being chased, swerving around corners, bashing into cars, it was time to surrender, the police had trapped us, they chased us down a cul de sac and blocked us in with several police cars. The chase was over. The police dragged us out of the car; I took one look at the car, and thought to myself, what a wreck. That car had lived its worse nightmare. Speedy and I were arrested and brought to the police station. I insisted, I knew nothing about where the car had come from, and as far as I was concerned the car belonged to speedy's old man, that's the god honest truth I told the police officer. I have to take my hat off to speedy though, because he did have the decency at least to tell the police officers that he did lie to me when he told me that the car had belonged to his dad. Because speedy was only fifteen at the time, and was under age, and didn't have any previous convictions, he was lucky, and got away with a slap on the wrist; sadly though, for the owner of the BMW, he was disgusted at the penalty given to speedy, and yelled at the police, shouting you cannot be serious!!!!!!!!!!.

This is a story about a poverish couple who knew each other from childhood sweethearts, and ended up going on to marry each other. They had gone through recessionary times together which made the potential for work extremely hard, it wasn't long before the bickering began and the strength of their relationship was truly tested. The situation was very tense at times and often resulted in very big arguments. This would be the beginning of a volatile relationship, and it continued for some time after, and often, Mary was left with black eyes and severe bruising. The funny thing about Mary and John's relationship was that they could go for weeks without an argument; there was a nice side to him as well you know; he would often do the best he could with the little he had e.g. John would buy Mary boxes of chocolates and he would often bring her flowers and send her cards saying I love you. But then there was this unpredictable side of him which was so violent; something I wouldn't wish on my worst enemy; this is where he would go completely berserk, I mean literally he would be insane and batter the hell out of Mary for no apparent reason other than that he might of had a bad day losing on the horses or being turn down for a interview or something so trivial you wouldn't consider to be that important; but for some strange reason it would be all John would need to fly of the handle. John finally got a job working as a welder and things were going well for about eighteen months until John was to learn that he was going to be made redundant because the firm he was working for were going into bankruptcy, as the cost of materials had gone up and the firms main trading customers were diverting into a complete new area where they would no longer be requiring John's services. The result of this would have a devastating affect on most of the firm's employees, as most of them were in their early forties and were married with two or three children who were still very much dependant on them. Things were tough and all the indication's looked as though they were about to get tougher. Anyway, the time was speeding ahead and before we knew it, there was only three months to go before John had to find himself a new job. John knew It was difficult enough getting the job he had let alone finding another one, and with the recession, who knows just how long it was going to be before he would find himself another. On top this John was to find out that Mary was expecting their second child; John's daughter Millie now aged seven was to find herself on the receiving end of one of John's tantrums, when one night John came home from the pub around twelve o'clock drunk as a skunk and woke Mary up from her much deserved sleep and started compelling her to make him a fry up, bacon, eggs, toasts and beans he said. Mary was completely dumbstruck by John's inconsiderate manner of asking her, or rather commanding her to prepare something for him in the early hours of the morning, which was totally and completely unreasonable; she had already made him his dinner for the day, but for some insane reason John did not want the steak which Mary had prepared for him earlier, which was in the oven, he wasn't interested in it, he wanted a fry up, and in a rage he threw the steak all over the floor yelling I wouldn't feed that to a dog. Mary started crying; John started shouting saying, I want eggs, bacon, beans and toast, and I want it now! Damn you woman. Mary refused to cook it; Mary was pregnant and was feeling really tired, and really did not have the energy to slave over the cooker at that time in the morning, so, Mary started walking away in the direction of the bedroom, when suddenly John came from behind her in one hell of a rage and grabbed her by the throat, squeezing the hell out of her neck screaming you refuse to obey my order? You refuse to obey my order!! Mary replied, I've already cooked you one meal for the day, as she replies in a sobbing manner, and if you want something else to eat you're just going to have to do it yourself. John opens his eye's wide and screams I dare you to say that again; Mary said it again, and John stripped off his belt and lashed Mary all over her face and body. Mary's daughter Millie heard the commotion and came rushing down the stairs to rescue her mother. By this time, Mary had collapsed on the floor; Millie picked her up escorting her to her bedroom saying to dad John you're an animal, how could you to treat mum like this? John replied "Animal" and boxed Millie in the mouth, bursting her lips. A month later and Mary had visited the doctors and was to learn that she had a miss carriage and lost her baby. Mary knew that this must have happened when John hit her when she collapsed to the ground. Mary was really upset by this and had gone into a deep form of depression; the result of which led to a lack of sexual feeling towards John; John couldn't understand why when he wanted to do it, she did not, and in his frustration he would box Mary until she did do it. Millie would often hear the noise but was wise enough not to get involved through her past experience. John had found himself a new job as a security guard and worked a shift late into the night and through to the early hours of the morning, and all he wanted to do during the day time was sleep. John was to get the shock of his life when one-day after having a drinking session at work he arrived home from work, and for no apparent reason whatsoever at all he started to hale a stream of abuse at Mary. Things had got to a boiling point when Mary was having a cup of tea, the tea pot was still very hot, and in a rage Mary threw the hot tea all over John's head; John ran off in a rage screaming ooh yah yah, ooh

yah yah, ooh yah yah, ooh yah yah. Mary knew she could not stay in the house because by the time John had cooled himself down he would kill her, he would kill her. So Mary left, and hid out at her mother's house. John knew that she would go there, and it wasn't long before he came looking for her. John came looking for Mary shouting from the streets calling Mary! I know your in there; standing at the door, Mary's mother replied go away, Mary does not want to see you; John replied, there is something important I need to speak to her about; it seemed as though he had calmed down Mary thought to herself? But wasn't totally convinced. Three weeks later and Mary decided she was prepared to take a chance and go back home, and to her surprise John seemed to have changed, acting more placid and calm. Mary decided that they both should go and get some professional counseling, they both agreed and gradually things started to improve.

THE DREAM

I woke up suddenly and there I was the centre of attention smack in the middle of a packed stadium, there must have been at least fifty thousand jeering fans there; I turned around and realized exactly what they were jeering for; they couldn't wait to see this enormous big black bull called Hercules maul me to death. As I slowly picked myself from off the ground, and there it was this big black beast with huge red eyes and huge nostrils with steam gushing out of them like crazy, steering at me in utter disgust that I had the temerity to be in the same ring as him, let alone the same stadium. I was terrified stiff. I turned around again and noticed a red towel laying on the ground; and just as I was about to pick it up, Hercules took four steps backwards then came charging at me like some raving maniac; can you imagine it? I narrowly dodged out of its way, it missing me by inches, god knows what damage it would caused had it had caught me. Anyway, it spun around doing somewhat of a ninety degree turn, and came back running towards me, it seemed all the more angrier for not having got me the first time. I watched on; and noticed the anger blazing through Hercules' head, and I just about had enough time to snatch the towel quickly. I could see how mad it was with me for not getting me the first time; it wanted to kill me!!!!!!!! But this time, as it came charging towards me I had the option of taken it by the horns or taken it by the balls, I took the balls, and squeezed the living day lights out of them, and there it was this so called big black bull called Hercules champion of the ring crying like a little baby. I had it all under control, as I watched him beg me for mercy. No more huffing and puffing and intimidating eyes, but complete subservience. It was as if it was pleading with me begging me please, please don't squeeze any more, I'll do anything you want please; ahh… I thought to myself you little baby, watching it lie down on its belly and allowing me to mount onto his back. I victoriously steered it out of the stadium; the crowd completely stunned; as they watched me triumphally make my way out of the stadium; they had never seen anyone come out alive with Hercules. They watched on in shear amazement of my victory.

THE BULLY

It was my first day at school and I was fully aware of my enormous size compared to all the rest of the kids. I knew it wouldn't be long before some wise guy cracked a silly joke about me and the rest would just join in like sheep. I knew if I wanted to get any respect around this place I would have to crack a few sculls together and basically scare them to death. The first couple of days went by smoothly and I was beginning to think that it was all in my head, until Michael Reynolds the snotty nosed ginger headed boy who always preferred to stay at the back of the class cracked a joke; I think he said something like bubba bubba, and everybody just belted out in this uncontrollable laughter; it was so.......... embarrassing, I felt so embarrassed, I felt two feet tall, and all because what that brat had said. I was determined as hell not to let him get away with it, and decided to duff him up after school; and to make sure I had him completely under manners, I got him to do me all types of chores, including stealing and bringing me money, every day. I had to do it, and I felt great! I felt like I was gaining my self-respect back. It was the day of P.E and I was absolutely hopeless at sports; I had hoped that they would have me excused from it, but oh no, everybody had to take part, and unless they had a medical reason for not doing it, everyone was included. Anyway, we had to jump over this horse, and I only landed flat on my belly smack in the middle of the horse, and everybody just belted out in laughter, it was so embarrassing.

I was 16 stone for heavens sake what do they expect; and I was only eleven, and had a chip on my shoulder. I didn't trust many people apart from my family, because they were all large in size too, and it wouldn't have made any sense in us cracking jokes at one and other, now that really would have been silly. Having a conversation with people proved to be difficult at the best of times, as I couldn't quite work out whether the person I was having the conversation with was speaking to me, or whether they were just gazing at me for my enormous size, thinking to themselves am I some sort of monster from out of space or something. The third day at school and the word had got around that I had been bullying Michael Reynolds; and a few of his pals were not best pleased that the fat guy (me) was taking advantage of their (chummy), so would you believe it, they planned to jump me after school, and did. But I was a lot stronger than the three of them put together, they were all weaklings; and I gave them a beating they would never forget, a beating of their sweet little lives. Before long, I had Michael Reynolds, Delroy Dennis, Tywan, and BabaTundy all doing different types of chores for me, I even got them to do my homework. It felt great!! What I hadn't expected was that about two months later Mr. Gleeson, my math's teacher asked me how I worked out the square route of 9, and for the first time in my life I was completely dumb stuck, I felt like a right plonker because I could not explain it. Once I had started this role of bullying the kids at school it became rather like a drug and as soon as I saw someone who I took an instant dislike too, I would just go up to them and thump them one in the belly and make some sort of excuse like, I heard what you said. That thump would usually be enough to have anyone surrender and hand over their belonging to me. I guess in a way I was becoming a type of monster, which had to be contained sooner rather than later before the whole thing got completely out of hand. Before long, I would have the whole school in fear of me and terrified of coming into school. Anyway, one day, I completely lost my rag, not with any of the school kids believe it or not, but with Mr. Levy, my English Teacher. He just kept going on about me not bringing in my home work in on time, so I told him, I'll bring it in stop bloody going on about it. Well, Mr. Levy was not best please about my manner of speech in which I used at him, and came towards me in one hell of a rage!!!!!! Well, that was it, as he came towards me, I thumped him one in the belly and he fell, out for six!! I was scared, because Mr. Levy was not getting up. Eventually, he did get up, and walked out of the class (or should I say stumble out of the class) and alerted the police. I was done for assault and expelled. It took me some eighteen months for me to be finally accepted into another school, which only happened to be eighteen miles away from where I lived, which was not only costly in getting there, but was a damned head ache for my dad who had to drive me there every morning.

THE BURGLAR STRIKES AGAIN

It was the third time in two years we had been burgled; my wife Mary and I was absolutely petrified of living in the house; we had lived here for the past fifty years. It was terrible; she would often cry for no apparent reason other than for the fear she had built up inside her from the ordeal we were having. The affect had taken its toll on Mary, and I had to be strong for the both of our sanity. Mary dreaded the moment it would happen again; and it got to the stage where even the sound of the postman putting a letter through the letterbox would be enough to sent shivers down Mary's spine. Mary kept asking me, why don't we just pack up and move away? But I wasn't going to allow some despicable pig; the satisfaction of running me out of my own home, why should I allow him to have that satisfaction? I know Mary wasn't happy, but my house meant a lot to me. I could never quite understand why we were constantly targeted; we weren't rich; I suppose our only real asset to the git would have been the television set, and what would he get for that £30; was it really worth it to cause us so much stress I kept on asking myself. Anyway, we had a good run without being burgled, and I was beginning to feel a little more relaxed and was beginning to think to myself it must have just been just a passing phase, everyone goes through it; when one night around 3.30am Mary thought she heard a noise, Bill, Mary called, Bill, wake up… Bill had been in a deep sleep, so Mary pinched him, and pinched him harder, but all Mary got was an even more heavier snore; Mary thought to herself oh my god how am I going to wake him up; so I blew down his ear, and he woked up; Bill, listen; we heard a clutter coming from the kitchen; it sounded like someone had knocked over the saucers left on the ledge; Bill got up, and stood at the top of the stairs calling out is anyone there, no answer; I stood behind Bill, terrified as hell. Bill cautiously made his way slowly down the stairs, then suddenly the cat appeared, meow!!!! meow!!!!!!!!! She murmured, I said to Mary it's only the cat. Then suddenly this tall man leaped out from around the wall, brushing me over, and running up the stairs, Mary screamed!!!!!!!!!!!Get out!!!!!!!!!!!!!!!! I shouted, come back here; and chased him up the stairs. Get out!!!!!!!!!!!!!!!!! He ran straight into our bedroom. Bill ran in after him; I heard the two of them fighting; I think he punched Bill in the head, but Bill continued fighting him; I screamed in terror as I watched the two of them fighting all over the bedroom, then suddenly, it appeared as though Bill was getting the better of him, and had got him in a half nelson; so I rushed up to the burglar and grabbed him by the nose and squeezed it as hard as I could, he screamed!!!!!!!!!!!!!!!!!!! Orr; Bill shouted, call the police, so I did, but as I was doing so, the burglar broke away from Bill's hold, and appeared to have the two of us to ransom. Bill shouted at him get out!!!!! He replied give me some money; Bill said all right, if I give you some, will you go? He said yeah, hurry up and give me some money; Bill said, I'll just get it, its under the bed, the burglar followed Bill, and just as Bill bent down to reach under the bed, the burglar bent down also, then to my amazement Bill pulled a hammer out from under the bed and wholloped him one over the head; the burglar ran off screaming Ahh….., holding his head. I called the police, and they caught him about a mile down the road holding his head, and nicked him.

I knew something was wrong by the way some of the girl's at school would look at me, then turn away and giggle. The very first day I joined secondary school, after about three weeks of continuous Mickey taking, I was beginning to loose confidence, and still hadn't found a friend; to tell the truth I was beginning to feel like a bit of an alien. So I turned to my nearest and dearest, my mother, for support, mother I said, the girls at school keep on laughing at me, and I just can't figure out why; mother replied they're only silly, take no notice of them, just keep yourself to yourself and do your home work, that's all what matters at the end of the day, it's your results that matters dear, your results. It was around five weeks into secondary school and I found myself a friend called Julie; she was such a nice girl, a little shy, but an angel. We got on brilliantly together, we helped each other out with each of our homework etc, and after about a month of knowing Julie, my confidence started to come back. I felt as though I could trust Julie, and confided in her, telling her of my experiences, and how I was being treated at school. I asked Julie if she knew why they were so mean to me, and why they were laughing at me. Julie took a good look at me; she took a while to answer, and hesitatingly, she told me why they were laughing at me. It's the hairs on your face Mary that's why they are laughing at you. Mary replied hairs, yes Mary, you know how fickle girls can be, that's why they're laughing at you; from that moment on, I could hardly bare to look at myself in the morning. I would just quickly brush my hair and teeth and take off for school in the mornings. Well, I can tell you, after hearing this from Julie; for the very first time in my life, I was made aware of how my physical appearance actually looked, and how it was so undesirable; it was a real eye opener for me. I suddenly realized how butch I was; I was beginning to feel like a female version of "Father Christmas," and became terrible self-conscious. One morning I plucked up the courage to face the mirror, and just held my hands to my face and cried and cried, I was so distraught with the fact that I hadn't bothered to pay attention to myself for so long; I suppose all the time I must have either been to busy or careless not to pay enough attention to myself, I guess I hadn't gave it much thought, and was really doing my best not to recognize the way I looked; because at the time it seemed so unimportant to me; anyway, I decided that I wasn't going to go into school that week, so I stayed off; mum hadn't realized that I hadn't been attending school because she left at 7.00am in the morning for work and she wouldn't normally be back until late in the evening; and when she left for work in the morning, she would normally just shouted from the bottom of the stairs, saying Mary I'm off, bye, I'll see you this evening, OK. It was a Tuesday, and mother had taken the day off because she had to go to the passport office to apply for a new passport, and was there to pick up the early post, and in amongst the mail was a letter from my school asking why I had been absent from school that week? After reading the letter, mother lost her rag!! Screaming and shouting at me; she did not know the real reason why I had been absent from school. She hadn't realized the taunting and name-calling and abuse I had put up with, it was unbearable, and I guess, it had taken its toll on me. After explaining to mother why I had not attended school that week, mother sympathized with me, and arranged an appointment for me to be treated by a top surgeon. The surgeon diagnosed the problem as a hormonal distortion of the skin, which was causing unnatural hairs to grow. Anyway, he prescribed me an ointment that repelled my facial hairs, it worked a miracle, and gradually my confidence returned, and the Mickey taking started to fade away.

It was the month of July and Todd and I were both on our school summer holidays together. We were so bored, we couldn't think of a damn thing to do; then Todd decided why don't we join up to a rowing club, I said brilliant idea Todd, and we joined up to Rower's sailing club. We went along and paid our fee and luck would have it that a canoeing trip had been arranged to the Lake District that weekend. Brilliant I thought to myself; I was so excited!! I could hardly wait for Saturday to come; it could not come soon enough as far as I was concerned, and although we didn't have to meet until 9.00am, I woke up at five that morning so excited about it all. Anyway, I knocked for Todd at eight, and you should have seen the excitement on his face; Todd made me a quick cup of tea, and we set off to the club, which was only fifteen minutes away. When we arrived at the club we mounted the awaiting mini bus, which left bang on nine-o clock, and headed straight for the motorway. On our departure some of the members started singing here we go, here we go, here we go. Everyone was in high spirit. We arrived at the Lake District at twelve o'clock, and by then all I wanted to do was just to get out of the bus so that I could stretch my legs. We got off the bus and headed straight for the clubhouse. We had a quick briefing from Terry the team leader about safety, and how lesser experience one's should keep close together. I had noticed the river was really rough in some places; Terry recommended we stook to the calmer parts of the river, but all I wanted was some rough and tumble, and that was exactly what I got. I saw some of the experience canoer's having a whale of a time, smashing into the rocks, it looked great! I wanted some of that I thought to myself. Todd seemed to be easy about being restricted to shallow waters; but that seemed awfully boring to me, so I branched off a little from Todd. Todd shouted come back Derek!!!!!!!! I branched off, deeper and deeper into rougher waters, to a point of no return. The river began to draw me into dangerous territory, and at this stage I had totally lost control of the canoe. Todd had quickly noticed that I was in trouble, and shouted for help! At first no one seemed to hear Todd, but bless him; Todd shouted and shouted until eventually someone heard. By this time I had capsized, and was rapidly been thrusted down stream; oh my god Todd screamed, oh my god, realizing I was in serious danger!! Todd spotted Terry and said this way! Terry came paddling speedily towards me; where is he Terry shouted to Todd? He's being swept down stream, quick, quick Todd pointed in the direction where I was heading; Terry immediately got on his radio to the rescue team, alerting them to where I was. By this time I was terrified!!!!!!!! I could see a cliff about fifty yards in front of me; I was terrified I would go over!! I looked up, and saw the rescue team on the bank shouting hold on!!!!! Micky the life guard threw me a tyre which was attached to a rope, I grabbed hold of it as tight as I could; thwu!!!!!!!! I gasped; I was saved.

It all started off when I got my BMW. It was a few years old but I loved it. What I hadn't realized was how much envy there would be towards my car and me. The attention I received was overwhelming. In my mind, I had hoped the attention I received would have been a positive one rather than one which was negative, but you can never tell these days. I thought I would have been alright getting a B.M; and I couldn't believe it when one morning I woke up only to find a whacking great big scratch down the side, I was devastated; I was furious; I kept asking myself who the rascal was it who did such an evil thing, I wanted to kill him. Three days went by and I was still baffled with who it was, who the devil was it? Who could be so jealous, so envious to do such a thing? I thought about it all day. I only had it a week, and had hardly driven it; and I there I was already thinking about an insurance job; and if I were to have it done on the insurance, it would have pushed my premium up three fold, so I decided to have it done privately; it cost me £400 big ones, but I had to have it done that way. I had to work overtime to pay for it, but finally it was it repaired. Doing it that way saved me in the long run, because it saved me from having my insurance premium doubled, to £1500.00 that would have crippled me. Anyway, I saved up and sacrificed my usual visit to the local, and after a couple of weeks, I muscled together the money and paid the garage; it was a pain in the arse, but I just closed my eyes and paid it. I thought to myself, its got to be a one off, it must have been some drunken bastard with a grudge or something, it won't happen again. Things couldn't have been further from the truth; just three weeks after I had it repaired, to my horror, the Git done it again, he vandalized my car again; I was devastated; I wanted to find out who the bastard it was, who was doing it, so that I could strangle him. So, I figured out, seen as though I was never around to see the bugger do it, I had to find a way of catching the Git, and of cause the thing that came to mind was a video camcorder. I would have him bang to rights; solid evidence I thought? So, I went out and bought myself a cam - recorder, and placed it in front of my top floor window, beautifully camouflaged behind the curtains, and have and behold, two weeks later the culprit suddenly appeared. I was shocked to realized that it was Mr. Thomas, my neighbour from across the road who used to say hello to me every morning; he had come out in the middle of the night; it must of been past two, like some deranged Demon from hell, with a vengeance; out to inflicted some malicious damage to my car; but this time, I caught the bugger, red handed. Apparently, Mr. Thomas had hated me from the moment I moved in; why, I dunno; but he did. I thought to myself why would he want to do such an awful thing? Was it because I wore nice clothes, or was it because I had a pretty girlfriend, or was it because I was always having fun parties and enjoying myself, and he just could not bare the thought of this young guy enjoying life? Perhaps his life was so sad, dull and boring, he hated to see people seemingly having it all, I just don't know. So, I guess he must have thought to himself, I'll have a go at him. Anyway he came out in the middle of the night with something which appeared to resemble a "Stanley knife" and gave my car another whacking great big scratch down the side!! But this time, I had him; he wasn't going to get away with it like he had done before. I had got him on film, and there would be no escaping this time.

Early that morning I brought the video to the police station and showed the officer just what Mr. Thomas had done. I had him bang to rights; and in the early hours of the morning, Mr. Thomas was given an early morning visit, and carried away to the police station. He was read out his rights, and nicked! At first he tried to deny it, but as soon as he saw his horrible "mug" on video, he soon changed his tune, and admitted it. The officer asked him why he had done such a cruel thing. Mr. Thomas's reply was that ever since I moved in, I acted like I owned the god damn joint; playing loud music all the time, having parties to all hours of the night; and his friends, leaving bottles and cans all over the street, I mean who does he think he is, ay. I've had it with him. I've lived here for twenty-five years and never had a problem with anyone until E came along with his loud music; I had to teach him a lesson.

And suddenly in the middle of the night from a distant, I heard a wild cat scream!!! It was two toms who had a long on going dispute over territory. The scream was so loud it made my hairs stand up on end. It was almost as if I had been struck by lightening or had an electric shock or something, and judging by the looks of both the ginger and black cat, their hairs too seemed as though it were up on end. Anyway the murmurs seemed to go on forever; then it would go quiet, then all hell would break out again, it was terrible! I saw scratches, bites, screams, you name it, it was hell out there. I only wished I could have stopped it; but they were at least four gardens away, and shouting from my fifth floor window at 3.30am didn't quite seem on. It seemed more sensible to just let them get on with it, and hope that it would fizzle out, sooner rather than later. Anyway, the fighting lasted about an hour, with it going off intermittently, then pausing and going crazy again; I mean really, these two blokes really had it in for one and other, and it seemed like neither of them wanted to back down. I'd have hated to have been the owner of either of the two, because I'm sure, neither of them judging by the screams and shouts I was hearing had escaped open wounds. Then suddenly after about an hour of madness, someone must have had enough. It was Mildred, a retired old lady who lived alone; she lived four gardens away, and I guessed the noise must have been unbearable for her. Anyway, I saw a light go on, and noticed her silhouette of a shadow appear in her garden; then I heard her shout shew! Shew! And in a second, the both the toms had took off in different directions; I guess, the disturbance had been quite enough for the both of them. The dispute would live to last another chapter. I was so relieved by Mildred's intervention, because I was beginning to think that the fight was going to last all night; you know like one of those retched car alarms. I eventually got my head down for couple of hour's kip.

SUSPICIOUS MINDS

I had been going out with Veronica for two years and things were great between us; but there was one thing I did notice about my relationship with Veronica, was, that if I looked at another woman, Veronica would absolutely go berserk, and fly off the handle; she would pinch me, kick me, swear at me, the lot. I would often say to her I'm only looking for heavens sake V; I don't want to go out with her or anything. Her reply would often be; well keep your bloody eyes to your self then.

Being in the music business I would often be surrounded by loads of women; It was just the way things were; try explaining that to Veronica; she would sooner have me in a job that I hated than be in one where I was happy and surrounded by women. But I loved my job, and couldn't imagine myself doing anything else. I also hated the fact that I had a jealous girlfriend, but what could I do? I wasn't going to get a job where I was unhappy just to please Veronica, because, I'm sure deep down, she would not have wanted to see me unhappy, and anyway it would be difficult to find a job paying the same salary I was getting. Anyway, what had happened was, after a long recording at the studio, the band had planned an evening in at my place for a change, so we piled up with food and alcohol. The evening was going ever so well, until Veronica appeared!! We hadn't arranged to see each other that evening, so I was a little shocked when she appeared. Anyway, she turned up and saw all of my friends, including a couple of girls; when Veronica saw this, I noticed Veronica's eyes light up!!! I guess, it must have been even more unbearable to see Sally and Jane sitting on my bed chilling out and talking about how the gig went that night. Veronica was a kind of a loner, and not really a particularly social type of person, in fact I believe that I was her only real friend, she was very much a homely girl, and really couldn't relate to the kind of lifestyle I had. Anyway, she came in, took one look and slammed the door behind her, and walked off. I ran out after her, and caught up with her some fifteen yards down the road and I asked her why she had left like that; what's wrong with you I asked? It's not what you think V, oh yeah she replied, I know what your planning on doing, I know, your planning on having an orgy aren't you, aren't you she screamed!!!!!!! No… Veronica we're just talking, just talking, and before I could utter another word she gave me one hell of a slap around my face, and walked off. Leaving me with my head spinning. The next day, I visited Veronica at work, at first she didn't want to acknowledge me, but I finally persuaded her to give me a second chance, much to her reluctantcy, I hasten to add, but she relented. That evening, I promised her I would take her out for a slap up meal to make up for it. We got to the restaurant, and I told her how much I loved her, and that she was the only one for me, and I wasn't interested in anyone else; she said to me, well, why do you have those bitches around your flat then? I replied, there's nothing in it V, you've got to trust me; you've got to trust me, you've got nothing to worry about, and with that said, she replied, I'm going to give you one more chance, you mess up, that's it. Three months down the line and the group were arranging a gig up town; and the only real way that we all could have met up, was at my pad, because it was central to where we had to go; but having forgotten about Veronica's ultimatum, I stupidly arranged this meeting totally oblivious to Veronica's threat; and just like the last time, Veronica turned up totally unexpectedly again; she rang the bell, dring dring, I asked Kate to get the door, because, Billy, the guitarist hadn't arrived yet, and I thought it was him; and to my horror, once again, it was "Veronica" Veronica took one look at Kate, and cut her eyes after her, and walked off. Kate returned to the kitchen where we all were, and I asked Kate who was that? She replied, Veronica, I ran outside, but she had gone. Fifteen minutes later, she was back, but this time, all I heard was ching a ling a ling!!!!! Veronica had found a brick, and had pelted it through my window.

I DARE YOU

It was the very first month of July and Eddie and I was on our school summer holidays together. Eddie, my mate, only happened to be a bit of a nutter; I mean the things he would come up with, like swimming in the hedges, he was crazy like that; and I guess I must have been equally as crazy, because as soon as he would jumped into the hedges and started swimming around, I would immediately jump in and do exactly the same thing, copying him somewhat. Eddie seemed to me to be having a whale of a time swimming in the hedges etc, it was almost as if he were in a different world. There was a time when Eddie invited me into his back garden and asked me to go and get his football from the other end of the garden which he booted down there, and he I asked me to go down there and get the ball, when to me my horror, Eddie pulled out an air rifle, and started taking pot shots at me, he was a bloody lunatic; fun to be with, because you wouldn't know with Eddie what was going to be next. Eddie continued to take shots at me; he was absolutely crazy. I yelled Stop! And shouted at him, as the pellets hit my body, it's not funny Eddie; he finally stopped when his mother heard my screams!!!!!!! She opened the window from the basement window, and shouted at Eddie, telling him to put that gun away; it's dangerous; the bloody idiot could have blinded me.
That afternoon Eddie reckoned he had a good idea; anything Eddie I said, so long as it doesn't involve taking pot shots at me. He replied, I promise it won't be you. All right then; what shall we do then Eddie? Eddie had planned on playing game hunter down the marshes; he reckoned there was a load of large rats and voles down there.
Anyway we got down there and as we were walking along the river bank and Eddie said shush… he thought he heard something. He did, it was this whacking great big rat; I was terrified of its size, I'd never seen one as large as that before; it was about the size of a cat; and certainly larger

than your normal domestic one; Eddie on the other hand had absolutely no fear whatsoever. As soon as he spotted it, he gave chase straight away, chasing after it like some raving lunatic, firing his air pistol at it like a "maniac" I watched on with shear amazement, as Eddie unleashed around some thirty to forty rounds after that rat, chasing after it like nobody's business down the river bank. I finally caught up with Eddie about some fifty yards away from where he left me. Eddie I called; did you get it? No, he replied, the dirty rat got away he said, I watched on as Eddie looked at me in somewhat of a look of utter disgust with himself for not killing it. The rat had dived into the river; don't worry I said to Eddie, you'll see another one. We started to walk slowly along the riverbank; it was silent as hell, when Eddie thought he heard a movement or a judder. I could see that Eddie was getting bored, and noticed his jaw drop somewhat into a hanging position; look, Eddie said; pointing at this huge pipe that spread across the river; yeah I replied; Eddie had planned on sitting smack bang on the pipe, right in the middle of the river; he thought to himself, he'll get a better view up there. Now, to get to the pipe we had to climb this huge wall which was about fifteen-foot, and then make our way across the pipe. I thought to myself this is crazy, one slip and we're history. Eddie just lunged up there as if it were nobody's business. I suffer from vertigo as a child, and also have a particular dislike for heights, and as far as I was concerned, going up there was insane and also totally ludicrous idea; to be frank, it's a complete bad idea, and down right insane. It's dangerous, I kept on saying to myself, it's dangerous. Anyway Eddie leapt up onto the pipe and sat smack in middle of the pipe yelling, Derek, come on up; don't be a "scaredy cat." I've got a good view up here he said; as he looked down on to the river, which was at least a thirty foot drop, and judging by the current, it seemed to be getting rougher by the minute. It might have all been in my mind, but when you're hanging around with someone like Eddie, you never know what's going to happen next. Anyway, I eventually gave into Eddies persistent calls, and slowly climbed up the wall, making my way to the centre of the pipe where Eddie was; I laid flat down on my belly; I hadn't the courage to do what Eddie had done, he just walked straight on to it; I was a bit more chicken than he, and crawled my way across. Don't look down, Eddie yelled. Don't look down; I took one look down, and said whay!!!!!!!! And turned round; scrambling my way back, when I heard Eddie laughing, hey hay, hay, hay hay, hay, and shouting out, you chicken.

This is a story about a violent man called Leroy, who murders his girlfriend Gina. Gina had a best friend called Rachel who she used to share a flat with, until Leroy killed her in one of his violent temper outbursts. Leroy had been fuming for quite a while about Gina's long hours at work and socializing with her male friends, when one afternoon everything just got on top of Leroy. Anyway, what had happened was, Gina was in her usual defiant mood about her working relationship with her male colleagues, and Leroy weren't having any of it; Leroy said to Gina, I'm going to tell you one more time; tell the F……ing truth, your seeing someone else aren't you? Tell the F........Truth; (Gina) or right then; you want me to say it; all right then, I am. It was to be Gina's last word. Leroy strangled her. Rachel had warned Gina about Leroy's violent behaviour towards her, but despite Rachel's sound advice telling Gina that she should leave Leroy, she stayed with him, insisting that she loved him, and that he would change. Leroy was arrested for Gina murder, but released on a lack of evidence. Leroy swore that on the night that Gina was murdered he was sleeping like a baby at his own flat. He said that on that night Rachel had been out with Gina and some of her Modeling friends, and the only thing he could think of is that some nutter must have murdered her along the way; Rachel was not convinced; she knew that Gina returned back to her flat, because Gina had called her not to long after she got in, Rachel had been visiting her mother that day. Rachel had turned up later that evening, only to find out that, that beast Leroy had strangled Gina to death. After the trial, Rachel was so appalled by the jury's decision she decided to get revenge; She wanted to show that scum "Leroy" that she knew he did it, and that he should always be on the lookout; Rachel decided to get him where it hurts; by damaging Leroy's most prized possession, his Jaguar xjs car. Rachel also knew where

Leroy drank; and waited for the "flash bastard" to turn up and go into the pub; she spotted him when he turned up, and as soon as he went in, she went up to his car smashed all the windows and scraped all over the brand new body work of Leroy's top of the range Jag. He was devastated. Leroy lived pretty close to Rachel, just a few hundred yards down the road, and within six weeks he had a new girlfriend; and Rachel would often see him holding arm in arm with his new girl, and carrying on like nothing had ever happened. No concerned whatsoever about the devastation he had left behind. He just carried on like normal, like nothing ever happened, the bastard. This new girlfriend of Leroy's ironically belonged to the same modeling agency as me; and the irony was, I found out that she had the same name as me, Rachel. Anyway, Christmas was just around the corner and our model agency was having its usual Christmas party, and we had both been invited. Rachel Gina's friend was seeing a male model called Jason at the time, and did not know he was friends with Leroy. ….. Anyway, it was the day of the party and Leroy had arranged to pick up Jason and his girl friend Rachel; you know turning up at the party as a four some kind of thing. At this stage, Rachel, (Gina's mate) had moved out of her flat and had moved to another area. Leroy had since then changed his car, and was sporting around in a brand new Mercedes Benz convertible; anyway, they arrive at Rachel's door with the roof down posing off like he always does. Jason leaps out from the back seat making his way to Rachel's front door, Leroy beeps on his horn beep beep, beep beep, beep beep. Rachel takes one look out of the window, and to her horror sees Leroy. She fly's down the stairs with the iron still in her hand, brushing passed Jason, Jason looks on perplexed; Rachel lunges towards Leroy like a raving maniac, and bolts him one around the head with the iron, and shouts from the top of her voice, F......off you F……..ing murdering scum you.

Bang bang, bang bang, bang bang. Bang! He was getting on my bloody nerves; what on earth can he be doing up there I thought to myself? What on earth can he be doing; after all it's a council flat not a blimming building site; I doubt whether he even works, he seems to always be doing something up there. Anyway, after several weeks of banging and clobbering, I was at my tethers end, and decided to have a quiet word with him to see whether he would quieten it down a bit, so I went up stairs and knocked on his door, and out came this enormous bearded man with a huge stomach who rather resembled" Grizzly Adams." Anyway, he opened the door with a hammer in his hand; I thought he was going to clobber me with it; I joked, what on earth are you doing in there; he replied, what's it got to do with you? I said to him, I live underneath you, and I can hear everything; the walls are only paper-thin you know, and its driving me crazy. He replied, well why you sound don't proof your walls then. I thought to myself what a bloody cheek; you inconsiderate bastard; and with that said, he said now, if you'll excuse me, I've got a lot of work to do, and he shut the door blam!!!! in my face. I walked slowly back down the stairs to my flat thinking to myself what a horrible and insensitive man. The noise kept on and on and on, and it got to the point where it was literally driving me out of my very own home, it was terrible!!! I would often go out of the house and walk around several blocks in hope that when I returned, the noise would stop. But what would normally happen was, just as I thought the banging had stopped, it would start again, bang bang, bang bang, bang bang. Bang!

I decided enough was enough; I wasn't going to allow this horrible man to drive me insane. I wasn't going to allow him to get away with it any longer. So I reported him to the local authority and they gave him a visit, and to their astonishment, Mr. Russell, would you believe it, was building a conversion without any written consent, or planning permission. The officer gave him a severe reprimanding and demanded him to break it down immediately. Mr. Russell asked the officer why they had visited him. And was told that there had been a complaint from one of the neighbours; oh yeah Mr. Russell replied. Mr. Russell was furious; after spending all his time, some six weeks building his conversion, and hoping that he would get away with it, only to have to knock it all down again. He was completely shell shocked when he was told to knock it all down, and was also warned that he would be getting another visit to see to it that he had done what he was told. That evening, I was rudely awoken up at 3 am in the morning, by one hell of a bang on my door, I thought it was a bomb; I leaped out of bed and opened the door, only to find this whacking great big sledge hammer lying on the floor; what had happened was, Mr. Russell had decided to get revenge, and came along, and gave my door one heck of a whollop and scarpered up the stairs. The dirty bastard.

THE FIGHTER

It all started off at the Crown & Manor youth centre, when Bruce got thrown out for continuously being caught smoking Marijuana. Bruce started to act strange from an early age of seven when his parents separated. He used to rebel a lot by striking back at his mother when she asked him to do the simplest of tasks around the house. As Bruce grew up, the situation got worse; the second week into Bruce's secondary school, Bruce got suspended for striking the Headmaster. Bruce had been caught smoking in the toilets. By the age of thirteen he was expelled and banned from the schools surroundings for setting fire to the woodwork class. Bruce was a solitary person who only had one friend called Scott, Scott was a talkative kind of a person, whereas Bruce was very quiet and timid, but had a vicious temper once triggered off, his good points were that he was honest, loyal and reliable, these qualities I believe Scott must had recognized in Bruce which was why Scott became good friends with Bruce. Scott would often save Bruce from being arrested by the police, because there were often times when the police would stop us and ask us questions, and Bruce would get all flared up, because he thought they were picking on him; and I would have to plead with the police officer not to take Bruce away. Bruce had such a fiery temper once he had been trigger off there would be no stopping him; he had such a temper he would rather die than to let someone take advantage of him or beat him up; and even if Bruce had blood pouring from all parts of his body Bruce would some how carry on fighting, he was crazy. In short he was a nutter. Bruce sometimes got into fights which had absolutely nothing to do with him; there was one occasion where we were drinking in a pub out of town and the publican refused to serve a drunken man another pint of beer, as his behaviour had been deplorable. He was caught squeezing lady's breast and telling their husband or boyfriend, you want to know! The man in question was this huge man, and seemed very confident. Anyway, whilst we were witnessing the dispute going on between the landlord and this ox of a man, it wasn't long before the whole thing came to blows; the landlord, an Irish man, who seemed to relishing in a bit of a barney was ready to go! And Bruce, for some strange reason, jumped straight in there throwing punches to the large man's belly; and although the large man had drank about fifteen pints of ale, and was as drunk as a skunk, he remarkably was holding up pretty neatly, and seemed to be in total control of his punches; he had quite a steady rhythm going on, despite of the some fifteen pints he had downed before getting all ratty, and had me feeling at times as thought he was going to rip the heads off both Bruce and the landlord. By this time passers by were witnessing the fight, and someone must have alerted the police. I saw the police car come whizzing round the corner; der der, der der, der der. So I quickly jumped in, broke Bruce off, and narrowly escaped through the back door. However Bruce did not come out of this frackar unscaved, his contribution to the fight which had nothing to do with him, was rewarded by eight stitches to his neck, he later claimed that it was only a scratch; a scratch I said! I realized that Bruce was not going to be accepted into any other school, and his education was pretty much doomed, so I decided to join Bruce up to a boxing gym, where Bruce does favourably well; he learns to fight professionally, and at the same time earns himself a respectful salary. There was one thing Bruce always dreamt of, it was to live in a proper house, instead of the rat cage of a flat which he grew up in. Bruce saved up his salary, and treated his mother, Ruth, for her birthday, a house with a garden. Ruth was so proud of Bruce. I mean the times when Bruce would get himself into blaze ups, and I would often be stood there feeling completely hopeless because I hated fighting, and would have been completely useless even if I were to have joined in, because I was terribly skinny, and would have looked rather like a bit of a rake, and totally odd looking; I always preferred negotiating my way out fights. (Unlike Bruce). So I focused on his strengths, and my brainpower. Meanwhile, whilst Bruce is rapidly climbing his way to the top, knocking the living daylights out of all of his opponents, and often within a matter of a few rounds, I knew a bit about business, as my father was a businessman, and was quite a shrewd type of a person. Myself, I was very good at making decisions and money transactions, and decides to become Bruce's manager; which I must say, I did favourably well, with 20% going to me and 50% going to Bruce, and with merchandising of 10% and television takings, we became multi millionaire's at a tender age of twenty three, life could not have been better.

I'M NOT TALKING TO HIM

It was the summer of 95, and what a scorcher of a summer it was at that; when one of my friends at work Mary and I decided what a brilliant idea it would be to have a dinner party out in the garden; that's a great idea I thought to myself; so we arranged it for Sunday at two. Mary had turned up prompt on time with her husband Jerry, and just as they were arriving, Steve my husband and I was just finishing off the salad, so I suggested to Steve if you and Jerry put the table outside, then Sue can give me a hand finishing off in the kitchen. Steve was only too pleased about the idea because it gave him and Jerry a chance to have a quick chat over a beer before the meal was ready. I could see from the kitchen window that they were getting along superbly, by the occasional sudden outbursts of laughter. I was a little hesitant at first as to whether they would get along, because at times Steve can be a little reserved; but they seemed to be totally relaxed in each others company, and things were going pretty much the way I planned it. It wasn't long before supper was ready; and I too couldn't wait to get tucked into the succulent mouth watering roast lamb which was cooling down on the side table. I looked at it impatiently, as the juices dripped ever so temptingly from its tender hide. The banquet was almost ready; and I could tell by the look on Steve's face that he too couldn't wait to get tucked in; he had a trance like gaze all over his face, so I knew that he was impressed with the fact that we had produce something that was going to be ever so delicious and tasty to eat. I asked Mary to lend me a hand to place the plates on the table; everything looked a delight; especially with all the garnishes and trimmings etc, it was just perfect. Half way through the meal, I couldn't believe what I heard; after all that time I spent slaving over the stove preparing such a wonderful meal; Jerry had the nerve to crack a wise guy joke about how my forks rather resembled pitch forks. I was incensed!

From that moment the atmosphere changed. I could tell by the look on Mary's face that she felt as though she was walking a tight rope.
I knew my forks were a little on the large size, but I hadn't really given it a thought. But, I certainly weren't expecting such a rude remark from Steve about me blooming forks. The next thing I heard was this sudden bust of laughter appear from across the table; it was so embarrassing. I didn't know whether to laugh, shrink inside of the woodwork of the table and die; or whether to say to him what a bloody cheek he had. I turned around and looked at Steve, and thought perhaps, Steve would have the decency to keep a straight face; but noticed instantly that he too was laughing hysterically like a blooming idiot; then Mary started; and before long, they were all laughing ever so hysterically, leaving me the only one not seeing the funny side of it; I remained completely straight faced. It was so embarrassing; me failing to see the funny side of things, but the only thing I could think of at the time was all the hard work I put into preparing the meal; all the peeling of the potatoes carrots etc, and all I get in return was a rude remark about something so insignificant as me blooming forks. I tried to change the subject, before I really did loose my rag. That didn't work either, because just when I thought they had sobered down and knocked the joke on the head, one of them would find the joke so irresistible and funny and start laughing again, stirring the whole god damn thing up again, like bloody idiots. I felt like telling the whole lot of them to get out!!!!!!!!!!!!!! Anyway, the evening was coming to an end and I couldn't help thinking to myself, I just can't wait for them to go; I wanted to give Steve such a rollicking for not having stuck up for me. He could have said anything; he could have said they're "antiques" anything rather than that bloody grin on his face, like a bloody idiot! So, I thought to myself, I know how I'll get my own back on him; I made out like I had a stomach cramp and a terrible head ache and that I wasn't

feeling too well; so I asked Steve to fetch me an aspirin, which I pretended to take, and asked him if he could do the washing up for me please darling. I knew Steve hated washing dishes, he despised anything greasy; I knew he would have really hated those greasy bowls; Steve took one look at them, and I could tell from his face that he was as miserable as sin, and what made it worse, he had to do it with his bare hands, because we were out of rubber gloves. I knew Steve couldn't be bothered to go all the way to the supermarket just for a pair of washing up gloves, and anyway, it was past ten o'clock, it's cruel, but it was the only thing I could think of to get my own back on him.

FRAMED

This is a story about a politician called Mike who is framed by the paparazzi whilst taking a picture of him in a restaurant with one of his long term female business associates, (Tina) whom Mike had done business with in the past and was about to clinch a multi million pound deal. Tina's boss (Steve) had appointed Tina to Mike. Steve knew they would get along and decided not to let her do the deal with her estranged ex partner Henry who work's for a sister company across the road who was seconded there, because Steve knew there was still some bitterness between Henry and Tina. Because Henry, Tina's ex boyfriend found out from one of their mutual colleagues that they were seeing each other and was furious. He had an suspicion that they was seeing each other, so Henry decided to hire his media paparazzi friend (Jerry) to keep an eye on them; Henry got to find out what there itinerary was, and knew when their next meeting was due, and informed (paparazzi man Jerry) where their next meeting would be. Jerry turned up at the restaurant and waited inconspicuously in the back of a van for that telling shot which would reveal it all, and would also net Jerry a couple of grand. In the past Jerry had a bit of a flurmish with Mike for taking an unwanted picture of Mike, and was repelled by Mike, Mike called him the scum of the earth; he left Jerry feeling somewhat embarrassed, and what was worse, Jerry at the time was new to his job, and it left him in feeling really low because he didn't realize how nasty the nature of his business can be, and really wasn't ready for that kind of slagging off from a politician. This time Jerry was ready for all types of abuse and had grown a thicker skin and was prepared for Mike's insults. Jerry took the picture he wanted; Mike spotted Jerry and rushed over towards him and shouted at him saying what do you think you are doing ay, ay, and lunges at the camera; Jerry responds, be careful, this is expensive equipment you know. Mike replies, I don't give a damn, you took a shot at me and I want that picture all right, all right. Anyway, the argument is temporarily ended, and Mike is about to leave, and just as he is about to leave, he kisses Tina in acknowledgement that the deal was done fine; and just as he looks around, Jerry takes another picture of him; Mike is furious!!! And Jerry shouts out to Mike, you don't even know how to organize a piss up in a brewery, let alone run a family. Mike is somewhat shocked by Jerry's comments and is somewhat astonished. Meanwhile ex disgruntled work mate Henry, still bitter that it was not him who was given the opportunity to do the deal with Tina, and really believes that it is he that deserves the bonus for all the hard work and contributions he sacrificed and made to the party was rewarded only with a demotion, and seconded to a junior position, not good enough, Henry keeps muttering to himself, not good enough? Just because I split up with Tina, Steve doesn't have to treat me like this? Meanwhile, Jerry happens to escape with half a dozen pictures of Mike embracing Tina and quickly disappears into the dark. Mike is so embarrassed by this because he had no idea that anyone apart from Tina was going to be at the restaurant. Mike run's out of the restaurant, giving chase after the Jerry, but its too late, Jerry takes off in a high performance car waiting nearby. Mike is so taken up by this; he returns back to the restaurant pays the bill and leaves. Mike decides he wants a bodyguard so he employs (Derek) Derek is having problems with his girlfriend Sue; they've been separated for years, but they still love each other and they have a little boy called "Pete" whom they both love dearly; Sue would like to have Derek back but neither of them has the confidence of asking each other to get back. Mike appoints Derek as personal assistant/private detective. He feels as though he could trust Derek because he's known Derek for a long time; they both played in the same football team together and felt he could trust Derek a lot more than any of his other associates. Mike later reads in the paper that how he was remembering the good old days with his ex-business partner and how he would like to get back together with Tina as a couple, and how Mike's marriage to Patsy is on the rocks, and destined not to last because for the past six years they've done nothing but argue with each other. Mike still loves his wife Patsy and realizes that this type of publicity is going to put yet another strain on his marriage. Mike explains the situation to Derek over a cup of coffee at his office. Derek explains to Mike that he is under a bit of pressure as well; because he knows he is wasting his life by not being together with Sue. Mike replies, well why don't you ask her to marry you? Derek replies, I don't know what she'll say, I mean, we haven't said a word to each other about anything like this in years. Mike replies, well, you never know until you ask, and the longer you leave it the harder it gets, and the more time you waste….. Mike suggests, look, leave it to me I'll see if I can sort something out and Mike arranges to meets Sue after work and explains to Sue the predicament Derek finds himself in, and how he finds it difficult speaking to her about such a sensitive matter like this. Mike asks Sue does she still love Derek. She replies yes……, but he was the one that left me not the other way round. Mike explains to Sue that at the time Derek was going through a difficult patch and did not know how to cope with the situation and found it difficult handling a relationship at the time because the loss of his job at the time made things even worse; and he needs you to forgive him for all the silly things he did; he also said that he doesn't know how to confront you about this, for fear that you will turn him down. He also needs to know if you would marry him. Sue takes a deep breath, and replies, how do I know that I'll be doing the right thing? How do I know he's not just saying this, and that he does really mean it? You should see the state of him Mike replies; take my word for it, he really means it. He needs you so much, and knows his life isn't worth anything without you. Mike says to Sue, look, this is what I'll do, I'll arrange a dinner for the both of us, I'll be there with my wife Patsy to take some of the tension off. Sue replies, you'll do that for me; you really would; …oh Mike, I'll always remember you for this, I'll remember this for the rest of my life. Mike replies, what are friends for. Meanwhile Mike is thinking to himself what's he is going to do about the pictures taken of him in the restaurant? Mike has a strong relationship with his wife (Patsy) they've been together for seventeen years, and they both trust each other, despite their rocky and sometimes turbulent past. Anyway, whilst reading the newspaper, Mike says to Patsy, can you believe this muck, look what some jerk has written about me; It's obviously a set up; someone's trying to frame me. Who would do such a thing Patsy replies; wait a minute Mike says to Patsy; no one other than that fool, that idiot who I used to work with along time ago who wasn't promoted because of his stupidity, and foolish ways would do such a thing, it's got to be him, he's got to be behind this; he thinks he's going to get away with it; I'll show him, I'll make a hole in his pocket so deep when I take him to court, he'll never think of doing such a foolish thing like that again. I'll sue him for libel, and make him and his stupid paparazzi friends business go bust; that'll show him not to fool around with people's marriages. What I'll do, I'll hire Derek as a private detective to find out all that he can about him, and what he's been getting up too; I'll get Derek to act as a plumber or a electrician or something, and place a bug in his phone, and find out all about what that that creeping little slime ball was getting up too, and get him arrested, that'll show him, that'll show him. Derek disguises his self as an electrician, bugs his phone and tapes him talking to Jerry about how his plan worked, and now he thinks Mike's marriage is almost certainly going to end in divorce; but Henry was wrong, because Mike's marriage is still very strong, and Patsy trusts Mike. Henry could not live with the fact that where his relationship went wrong, Mikes one was still very strong, and despised him for it; and on top of that, he had the temerity to be seen kissing his ex girlfriend Tina. That isn't on Henry keeps muttering to him self. That isn't on.

GUZUMPED!

I'd been looking for a pad for months when I finally saw one I liked; it was in need of a little bit of decorating, but that was all; I suppose I was reasonably happy with my find, so I put in a offer with the estate agent. After filling out all the relevant forms etc; everything seemed pretty rosy; the gentleman who was dealing with me (Mr. Jones) seemed more than happy at the time to process my application. We shook hands, he smiled, and I thought to myself what a charming man; what I hadn't realized was that, that creeping little slime ball only put my application on the back burner, and didn't really process it, instead, he was hoping that someone else would come along and offer him more money. When I left the office, Mr. Jones said to me that he would call me within two weeks to confirm that everything was all right. I waited, and waited for that phone call "Jonesy" promised me, and after three weeks of not hearing a whisper, I decided I would go down there and find out what that slimey little slime ball had been getting up too, only to hear of his lousy excuse telling me that the owner had decided that he wasn't selling anymore; the lying little scum bag. I met the owner by coincidence when I bumped into him whilst he was putting his garbage outside; the owner assured me that his house was still up for sale. The following day I noticed a removal lorry parked outside the house. I asked the removal man what's going on ere? He replied, oh, the young lady inside has just moved in and we're moving in her stuff. I was absolutely livid, and confused. I couldn't quite figure out what was going on, and stood there for a moment or two scratching my head. The lady which had just bought the house came out singing, oh what a beautiful morning, oh what a beautiful day, oh what a beautiful morning, everything is going my way. I confronted her immediately asking her what does she think she was doing. She replied, I'm moving in my dear. Now please, if you don't mind, please excuse me, I'm extremely busy, and carried on her with her business, I was absolutely job smacked. I wasn't particularly angry with her, but absolutely furious!!!!!! With that scumbag (Jonesy), the dirty rat had betrayed me, how could he do such a thing to me, I trusted him; I kept saying to myself, I trusted him. The dirty rat, how could he do this to me I questioned myself as I walked back home. I just couldn't wait to see that pig; so, I hurried home and dropped off my shopping in the hallway of my flat, and sprinted down to the office. I arrived just in time, because they were just closing up for the day, when I spotted "Jonsey" getting into his flashy BMW car, he had one leg hanging out precariously, speaking to someone on the phone, I ran up to him and swore at him, calling him just about every name under the sun, he replied, what's the matter luv; he was acting like butter wouldn't melt in his mouth. I told him don't give me all of that you know what you've done you pig; he tried to act like I had it all wrong; I said you're damn right I've got it all wrong, and slammed the door on his leg, leaving him screamed awooh!!!!!!!!! And I walked off.

And the dreaded thought of Uncle Johnny turning up in his usual drunken and pathetic condition terrorized my state of well being. What's it going to be like this time I thought to myself, vomit all over the carpet, a blaze up of an argument with daddy over some minor dispute, or will he do what he normally does and pretend that he cannot find the toilet, and decides to himself that his sacred urine is far better for the daffodils rather than natural rain water. Anyway, my curiosity couldn't hold up any longer, and I just had to find out exactly where Uncle Johnny had disappeared too. His elusiveness had got my curiosity going, and I couldn't help but to spy on him; if only, for his safety. It appeared that he must have wanted some fresh air, but couldn't be bothered to tell anyone where he was going; this left me somewhat concerned. Anyway, he some how made his way out into the garden. Although I thought I heard him murmur something like this, ….I'm going outside, but it wasn't very clear; and just as I predicted, my curiosity was spot on; I took one look around the corner, and watched on in horror, as uncle Johnny, hardly being able to hold himself up, and hanging rather precariously with one hand leaning on the fence, in the pitch of the dark, pissing all over the garden plants, and it also appeared, all over his shoes as well. Uncle Johnny I shouted! He pretended not to hear me, whilst he drained himself off, which seemed at the time to be a whole fifteen minutes long. Uncle Johnny I shouted! You can use the lavatory you know you don't have to pay for it, I said to him sarcastically. He muttered, I'm coming inside, I'm coming inside. He stepped in the house not even bothering to wipe his muddy wet shoes from where he was standing in the dirt, and swayed his way through to the kitchen leaving his tracks behind him; and finally making his way through to the lounge, where he just collapsed onto the settee; legs wide open, and arms on his lap. I offered, or rather insisted on making him some black coffee; whereby, his reply to me was, "black coffee," I hate black coffee, I don wan no black coffee. I offered once again; Uncle Johnny, I think you need one. And just as I was about to put on the kettle, I noticed Uncle Johnny reach into his inside jacket pocket and reveal a half-empty bottle of Vodka. I said to uncle Johnny, don't you think you've had enough; and with that said, his eyes lit up in anger, yelling who the hell you think you are telling me dat I had enough, sacway copawayzoar he replied in his patois native West-Indian language. And took a swipe at me, narrowly missing my head, and mumbled, move out my way child, let me go home you hear he muttered to himself, I just watched on, as he staggered his way through the hall and out of the front door. THANKS GOD he's gone I said to myself. THANKS GOD he's gone.

It was my very first time abroad, and where we were located, we had such a panoramic sight. The weather was fantastic, and the people were ever so hospitable and kind and I guess the only thing next for me to do was to find myself a knight in shining armour, and that was exactly what I found. There he was this tall dark and extremely handsome man; to be honest with you, I just could not believe my luck; it was just like a dream. His parents owned a restaurant and he was head waiter.

That evening, my friend patsy and I were out for a night out on the town. But first, we stopped off at Stephno's food & wine restaurant for a simptulating bite to eat, because we knew that in the heat of the night we would not get hungry, and we would be able to sustain an all night rave. Anyway, we arrived at Stephno's, and as we entered the restaurant, I noticed instantly the décor, and how beautiful the place was; it looked absolutely stunning; there were Van Goff painting on the walls, crystal chandeliers, the place was a dream. We started off with a light bowl of soup, just to get us in mood, coupled by lobster, and finished off with a cau de Blanc white wine. The meal was everything you could have wished for, and more. It wasn't long before Derique, the tall dark and handsome waiter came over to find out if there was anything else he could get for me, Madame he said, maybe a taste of our very own home ice cream, or our very own pino colado he offered; my mouth, still watering having seen this tall dark looker of a waiter come over to me in such a seductive manner, had me gasping; anything you recommend my darling I replied.

Certainly Madame he replied. He gazed straight into my eyes with his big brown eyes; I was totally besotted by him. It wasn't long before the ice cream had arrived, and Derique suggested a little more wine Madame? Yes please darling I replied; and watched him pour the wine into my glass ever so slowly and with such elegance. I couldn't help thinking, does he do everything in such a seductive style. Anyway, we finished our wine, and Derique came over to us, and asked us, is everything all right Madame? I replied your service was absolutely super, and gave him a ten-pound tip. Derique responded have we got anything planned for tonight? I replied nothing in particular my darling; he swiftly replied how about a night-cap, in front of the beach, in front of a fire, and some gentle music. It sounded like paradise. I found out later, that it was a customary thing they do for there night caps; so, we took up on Deriques brilliant suggestion, and listened to him whilst he told us everything we needed to know about the culture and the best places to visit; which of course his place was amongst the list. Later that evening Patsy was feeling a little tired and wanted to get her head down; she wanted to have a proper lie down in her bed, and digest properly the heavenly food and wine we just had, and made a subtle hint that her bed was calling her. She could sense, that Derique had eyes for me only. Patsy went up to her room, which was just across the road, and Derique and I lay in a dangerously seductive position on the sand, and spoke intimately to one and other. The feeling was very romantic. Derique noticed that I was feeling a little cold as we watched the night pass us by, and rapped his blanket he had brought out with him around me, and played me a favourite song of his on his guitar. We stayed up until the very early hours of the morning, and just as the sunset began to rise, we decided to go inside. Derique walked me to my bedroom; then asked me, if I would like to come to the magic gardens with him later that afternoon, and that was where he knelt on one knee, and asked me to marry him. My obvious reply was, yes, yes, yes.

YOU BLOODY HOOLIGAN

It was a Saturday afternoon, and I decided I wanted to go out and watch a football match, so I went over to the marshes, and when I got there, there were several teams playing, but there was this one team in particular, which took my attention; I found out later that the team what I was watching was called the Blue Arrows, and they were playing the Eagle hearts; they were both pub teams. Anyway, I was pretty impressed by the standard of the football, considering the image one would have of pub team, you know the typical group of lads with beer belly's running around the place. Well, some did have beer bellies, but on the whole they were pretty good, and appeared to be quite organized; and the Arrows, they had this centre forward who was like lightening, and every time they passed the ball to him, he would leave the Eagles defender for dead, and put the ball in the back of the net. Anyway, half way through the second half one of the Eagle's players chopped down one of the Arrow's mid field player, and from that moment on the temperament of the game went down hill; in fact it was down right appalling; and every so often you would hear from one of the fifty or so crowd which was there supporting the Arrows hale a stream of abuse at the ref. shouting out, the referee's a wanker! The referee's a wanker! The Arrow's supporters were being abusive at the referee because they felt as though the referee was on the Eagle's side, and did them an injustice, when he failed to book or send off the Eagle player for that suicidal tackle he made on the Arrow's midfield player. The Arrows started off the match as the underdogs, but by half time they were already three nil up; much to the Eagle's disappointment, they were expecting to give the Arrows a thrashing, but much too their disappointment, they were the ones getting the thrashing, and it seemed almost at times that the Arrows were making a mockery out of them, I mean the Eagles were meant to have been top of the league, and at times I would hear from the sidelines the Arrow's supporters singing "Olay" "Olay" I have to admit, they were rubbing it in a bit, and trying to make it look easy. It was a classic situation where the bottom of the league team was playing the team at the top of the league, and the team at bottom of the league was making the team at the top look stupid. I mean how often do you see that ay. I could sense something terrible was going to happen, when the Arrows scored a fourth goal, a minute from the end, and the ref was getting ready to blow the final whistle. I could see the Eagle's fan were beginning to get restless, and agitated, when suddenly I saw this Eagle fan, with a beer gut, rush onto the pitch, grabbing the referee by his neck, and dragging him half the way across the pitch, It was hilarious, he was so angry!!! I thought to myself this guy is a maniac!! And before I knew it, the rest of the team started fighting with each other on the pitch, it was horrible. After about ten minutes of shear madness, kicking, thumping, F in and blinding, and god knows what else, they relented and went back to the changing room to get dressed. I dread to think of the language they must have been using in there; but all I know is by the time I got back to my car, switched the engine on, this nutter suddenly appeared and started jumping all over my roof; I think he must of thought I was one of the Arrow's supporters. I wound down the window of my car, and screamed, get off my car you Bloody Hooligan. Get off my car.

The bombing of a high society nightclub: It all started off one Saturday night, Todd, Jerry, Micky and I decided we wanted to go out and get pissed out of our heads, so we started off drinking at a few local pubs, played a few games of snooker and darts and then went on to get a bite to eat; we then went on to a few more pubs; at this stage we were all a bit tipsy as you can imagine; we must of all had about fifteen pints by that time, and anything anyone tried to tell us really didn't make a lot of sense at the time, because, by then as we were all completely stoned. But despite being completely stoned, I was the only one who could walk and talk straight, although technically, I was out of it. Anyway, after we had our last drink, we decided we wanted to get some girls; and being that the pub we were drinking in had nothing there but an old stripper and the bar lady, who was the governor's missus, we decided to go to a nightclub. So we got a taxi and stopped off in Soho, West End. There were all types of characters down there; prostitutes inviting us to go into their peep shows, the lot. There even had gay clubs inviting us in. Anyway we passed on all of those and went to a nightclub called Pal Joey's. Unknown to us, there were four guys pretty similar to us who were making a scene outside the club, spitting on the cars going by, grabbing other guy's girls and trying to kiss them, causing a terrible scene outside the club. All this was happening whist the bouncer was witnessing it all, it wasn't long before the louts tried to get into the club. The bouncer's obvious reply was certainly not in ere mate! And In a sudden one of the guys pulled out a bottle he was drinking and smashed it over the bouncer's head. Pandemonium broke out!!!!!!!. The girl in the reception called some of the other bouncers who were downstairs; they came up, and gave the guy who smashed the bottle over the bouncers head one a hell of a beating. Anyway, after they had beaten him until he was black and blue, they returned to see how their bouncer friend was doing; (Tom) the injured bouncer had only been in the job for a couple of weeks, and was very new to the job. Anyway, what they did, they rushed Tom to the hospital. By this stage, Todd, Jerry, Mick and I was just arriving, and the manager of the club was at the door, he was a greedy type of guy who was only interested in money and letting in as many people as he could; his only interest was to get rich, so getting in was a piece of cake. By this time we were all on our second round, and we heard one the bouncers say that Tom will be all right, and had returned home with 5 stitches. The time was 3.30 am, and there was about two hours to go before closing time. So, by then we decided we had had enough, and decided to go home. And as we were going through the door, one of the bouncers looked at Todd suspiciously, as he thought Todd looked pretty similar to the thug that had bottled his bouncer mate, Tom. And just as we were making our way through the doors we noticed a guy with an Arsenal hat on drive up to the club and get out of his car and walk to the rear end of it, and out of sight. We thought something was strange because at that time everywhere else was closed, and the only place to really be was in the club. What he had done, he'd planted a bomb in the car, and went back to his friends, who were waiting in another car, a few yards down the road. By this time, it was a round 4 o'clock and people started to emerge from the club; and were basically just hanging around like night clubbers do, chatting. Then in a sudden one of the gang said "Now!" He must have thought he'd recognized the Bouncer, the one who gave him a black eye. So he pressed the button to detonate the bomb. The bomb went off bang! Shattering all the windows of the nightclub, and a few other shop windows, seriously injuring ten people, including the bouncers. The police were there in a matter of minutes, as were the fire engines. Everyone around was totally in shock. The news reporters were there. The ambulance came and took around 25 people to hospital, treating them for minor injuries and shock. The next day the police started to narrow up a few important witnesses, and asked people whether or not they had seen anything strange or peculiar happening. The receptionist was a key witness, as were two couples who were in the club when the guy with the bottle glassed the bouncer. Anyway, they narrowed it down to Todd; I think they must have given a description of Todd, as they thought Todd looked pretty similar to one of the thugs. They arrested Todd, because he was spotted on the video camera in the nightclub. Todd has a record for GBH when he was a youth, but hadn't been in trouble since, he had changed, and was a reformed character. They said he was the one who bottled the bouncer in retaliation for not being allowed into the club, and said he decided to get revenge by causing serious injury to the club and the bouncer. They took Todd away and locked him up for 10 years. We were all absolutely devastated. We were not going to let it rest at that; no way. So we decided to do our own investigation to find the culprit who was responsible. It took us 18 months before we finally tracked down the bouncer who had been glassed, because he had returned to his native Yorkshire, and decided he was giving up bouncing all together, after the ordeal he had. We asked him if he would come to the prison with us to positively identify Todd as not the one who had glassed him; He agreed, and did so. After about six months, Todd was released and the police search began to track down the real perpetrators. They found them by chance; when the receptionist was out doing her local regular Sainsbury's shopping, when she noticed the same guy with the same Arsenal hat on. He was doing his shopping with his girlfriend. So the receptionist followed him, and took down his address and gave it to the police. The police arrived at his house, plain clothes with the receptionist girl (Jenny) in a car, with blacked out windows to protect her identity. The police rang the bell, the scum bag opened the door, Jenny said, that's the one, by pressing an alert button which was given to her to signal to the police that they had the right one, and they arrested him. They brought the bouncer guy down to identify him; Tom positively recognized him as the one. The police checked out his history and found out that he was an expert on explosives, and had actually been caught once before, but released on lack of evidence, but not this time, there was too much evidence, forensic evidence of finger prints on the car, and his ugly mug also on camera. Despite being positively identified, and caught on camera, and being the one involved in causing such terrible injury to the bouncers; despite all the evidence, the accused still had the temerity to go for not guilty. He was convicted and jailed for 12 years; and just as the judge were about to sent him down, he stuck his two fingers up to the judge; calling him a miserable old bastard, the judge was incensed, and gave him an extra 4 years for descent.

I CAN'T STAND IT

This is a story about a sixteen year old boy, who has a big problem with his father for bringing home his long term girlfriend and allowing her to stay over night. Derek's father had warned him several times before about this, but despite of Derek's warnings Derek is still prepared to take risks. His passion for Carla is so strong; he feels he needs to be with her all night. One night, Sam, Derek's father, came home quite late from the pub, and heard Carla's screams of passion coming from Derek's bedroom! Sam was furious, as he had warned Derek several times before about this, and Derek had disobeyed him once again. In anger, Sam strips off his belt from around his waist, rushes up the stairs, in one hell of a rage, busts straight into Derek's bedroom, and started lashing out at the two of them. Derek and Carla start screaming I'YIH YI, I'YIH YI, I'YIH YI.

They managed to make a quick dash for it out of the bedroom, and down the stairs. It was so embarrassing for Derek; whilst being caught up in his love making. He totally forgot about his previous warnings; I guess the passionate must have been so overwhelming. Derek felt so ashamed of himself; and found it difficult to come face to face with his father, so he decided to stay away from home for a couple of weeks. Derek thought to himself if I stay out of his way for a while, Sam would have calmed down, and then he would be able to face him again. Three weeks passes by, and things are back to normal, and Derek just about manages to say ….good morning daddy hence, a minimal amount of conversation. Sam worked very long hours in the steel factory, and really didn't put time aside to spend quality time with his four children; I guess his excuse would have been, I work too hard. But I'm sure with a little bit of careful planning, he could have done so, but he weren't particularly bothered. He spent all his leisure time down the pub. I'm sure with a little thought and attention, he could have managed to spend some quality time with his four children, who all long for his love, affection, and attention, but they never received it. I figured out, the thought perhaps never even came into Sam's equation. Six weeks down the line, and Derek's is still seeing Carla. And despite of what they had both been through, they're still together; and the irony is Derek, assures Carla he knows the pattern of his dads Sam's shifts, and squeezes Carla in, when he thinks Sam will be at work. Realizing that he could probably get away with it, Carla agrees to spend the day. Convinced that there won't be any interruptions this time, from either mother or father, who are both supposed to be out at work, (Julie) Derek's sister is at college, and is not expected back until late afternoon; Jake and Perry are away on their school summer holiday trip, so he says to himself, I won't get caught this time. Derek explains all of this to Carla, who believe it or not foolishly believes Derek; she allows Derek to convince her that everything will be awright!!! As he reassures Carla; and say's to her, so long as we get up by 4pm, everything will be awright, Trust me. Carla takes a gamble, bunks off college, and plans on spending some quality time with Derek. They make love, and fall asleep; and once again they end up being totally being oblivious with the timing, they make love several times, again, and again, and before they knew it, the time was fast approaching 4pm!!!!!!!! And Sam had arrived a little earlier than expected. Sam would normally go down to the pub for a few pints before returning home, but this time, Sam was feeling a little tired from his hard day at work, and returned home a little earlier than expected, and just as he's about to crash down on the sofa, and snooze off, he's only awoken once again by Carla's screams!!!!!!!!!!

He's furious, he's raging, he's angry. He strip's off his three inch thick leather belt, holds it up buckle side up, fly's up the stairs, kicks down the door, punches and beats the two of them up. Derek and Carla fly's down the stairs petrified as hell, and onto the streets; both completely naked, and feeling somewhat embarrassed. Sam slams the door behind them, and reaches for his bottle of whisky, to calm his self down. He flings his self down on the sofa, mad as hell!!!. Meanwhile, Derek and Carla hide's behind the bushes, a few yards down the street, waiting desperately for his sister Julie, to return home from college, so that she could get them their clothes. Derek and Carla had to wait behind the bushes completely naked for one and half-hours, before Derek finally spotted Julie, strolling down the road. PS!! Derek whistles from behind the bush! At first Julie is stunned, but when Derek calls again, Julie, recognizes her brother's voice, and says, Derek what are you doing behind there? Derek explains his ordeal, and how he was caught in the bedroom with Carla, and how he was belted out of the house, and onto the streets, without any clothes on. Julie giggles; (Derek) don't laugh Julie, its not funny; Julie notices Carla, crouched behind Derek, with a half giggle look on her face, but realizes that they really are as embarrassment as hell; Derek says to Julie, I need you to creep into my room and bring out our clothes for us alright Ju. Julie replies what if he sees me? (Derek) he won't see you, just creep; Julie open's the front door with her key; (Julie) Sam shouts, Julie! Is that you? Yes daddy, she replies, trying her best to pretending that she hasn't seen Derek, and desperately pretending that she doesn't know about anything about what has gone on; Sam asks Julie, have you seen that Derek? No daddy, I haven't, as she sneaks into Derek's half-open bedroom, and grabs hold of the clothes she spots hanging on the chair. (Julie), I'm just going to the shop dad; I've forgotten to get some tip ex; she stuffs the clothes into her shoulder bag, and dashes out of the house; back in a minute dad. She hands the clothes over to Derek, from the other side of the bush; Derek breathes a sigh of relief, and say's to Carla, what a relief. Derek knows he cannot go back to the house, because Sam had given him his final chance. He has no money, and neither has Carla. Derek's not expecting his "Giro" for another two-week's because he spent his entire previous giro on a pair of Reebok trainers. Derek left school two years ago when he was fifteen, and finds it hard in getting a decent job, due to his lack of qualifications; and Carla who is sixteen, and really should be at college, they find themselves in a right pickle. Anyway, Derek spots his neighbour Donald & Sarah, coming down the road with shopping bags; it looked as though they had been doing a spot of shopping down the market. Donald calls, Derek; and says how are you? Do you fancy coming in? Where having a Barbie," Derek and Carla both go into Donald's house, Derek refrains from telling Donald about what has just happened to him, and just chats away as normal. Whilst Derek is busy chatting away to Donald, he notices Carla ponse a cigarette off of Sarah, and is furious with her, as she did not even wait until Sarah offered her one. And on top of that, she hardly even knew her. Derek is so desperate at this point, he doesn't even know where he's going to sleep tonight, and decides to do something totally out of character and smashes a jewellery shop window, grabs the most expensive item he sees, in hope that he could sell it, and pay for a bed and breakfast lodge. Right, so he grabs this £3,000 necklace, sells it down the jewellery store, and is able to buy some time for a few weeks. The story goes that he smashes the shop window!!!!!!!!!!!!!!!! Snatches the jewels, and runs for his life!!!. The alarm goes off, the shopkeeper comes out running after him; and yelling stop that thief! Derek sprints around one corner and then another, and luckily enough spots a bus pulling away from the bus stop. He jumps on, looking out through the window, he spots three police cars come whizzing around the corner, sirens screaming out like nobody's business, heading in the direction of the shop. Derek, still shaking like a leaf, whilst sat there on the bus, looking out the window, petrified as hell!! Only to be confronted by the bus conductor, who scares the living daylights out of him, by yelling fares please! Derek has no money, and asks the bus conductor does this bus go to Victoria? Knowing full well that Victoria is in the opposite direction, and the bus is heading in the direction of the Angel, which is actually in the direction he wants to go, and manages to stay on for one more stop, which lands him more in the direction where he wants to go, and closer to the bed and breakfast where he's staying. The following morning Derek takes a stroll out with Carla down the High St, and notices his face plastered all over the television on "crime watch", saying, have you seen this man? By coincidence, an estate agent, happens to recognize Derek, and calls the police; they arrest Derek, and he ends up with a criminal record. Derek's father Sam, is so upset by it all, he allows Derek back into his house. Sam finds Derek a job at his work place, and Derek saves up all his money, put a deposit down on a flat, a couple of yards down the road, from the family home, and is able to spend quality time with his love of his life Carla, without and complications.

He made me do it; I didn't want to kill him; he tortured my life by always being around, and even when he weren't actually there, he would always ring or turn up out of the blue. He turned my life upside down for months by keeping on turning up out of the blue, time after time; after time; why wouldn't he just stay away, and cut off his connections with Kate all together; she was going out with me now, not him; why wouldn't he just leave us alone to get on along with our lives. He wouldn't do it; he just had to keep coming round.

I loved Kate dearly, and I'm sure she loved me too. I know she had feelings for Tommy, but she knew she couldn't trust him; he was always having affairs whilst he was with her, and she knew he would always let her down. Tommy would always have several girls on the go at the same time; Kate was so naïve, and it would appear that she really didn't consider my feelings seriously enough; despite the fact that we had been seeing each other for six months, and deep down, I believe that she knew that it was I who really loved her, and I, was the one who would be loyal to her, not him. Anyway, what had happened was, we had been out to a party together, and the time was about 3.30am in the morning; we were both tired, and all I wanted to do was go to sleep with Kate. But who was it; who was it who decided to be a bloody nuisance, (Tommy); he was waiting outside Kate's house for three hours in his car, and when he saw us coming he jumped out of his car and called out Kate; and would you believe it, Kate just left me as if I weren't even there, and went straight over to him; I was livid; I was absolutely furious!!!!!!!!!!! I warned her to break connection with him; but would she listen to me, oh no.

Well, Kate started talking to him, and acting as if I weren't even there; I was totally green with anger!!!! I felt like the "Incredible Hulk," I wanted to rip Tommy's head off; and what made things worse, he had the bloody nerve to say to me goodnight mate!! Indicating, that it was him who was going to bed with Kate that night and not me; well, that was the final straw. I leaped onto his back, and gave him one hell of a kick in the nuts, and fell to the ground; and I said to him goodnight mate! And opened the front door, and slammed it behind me. When I got inside, I gave Kate one hell of a hiding, for embarrassing me like that. One hour later, and Tommy was back kicking and banging on the door; I ran over to the door, angry as hell, that he had not got the message the first time, and to my horror, Tommy had a gun, and was pointing it at me, I said to Tommy, put the gun away Tommy, don't be stupid; he said to me, the only one who's being stupid is you, pointing the gun at me; the commotion started to get a bit loud, and Kate's next door neighbour who lives across the road heard the shouting, and came out to see what the hell was going on; and just as Tommy span around, I quickly jumped on him, grabbing the gun; the gun went off, bang! I had shot Tommy in the belly, and he died instantly. I went to court and was charged with Tommy murder. I didn't mean to kill him.

INHIBITIONS

This is a story about an anti social student who happens to share a house with four girls and four guys. The student lifestyle is typical where the customary pattern is to go out regularly together to pubs and clubs. Derek strikes curiosity by not going along with the rest.
Derek's colleagues just can't understand why Derek won't come out with them. Derek often tries to explain to them that the reason why he doesn't go out is because of his phobia of being in strange places, and that's what inhibits him. Derek explains this to his closest mate David. This inhibition of Derek's has made him a type of recluse and ultimately makes him miss out on an awful lot on his social life; it also made it quite difficult for David not knowing quite what to do. David always tried to encourage Derek but to no avail, this inhibition of Derek's almost destroyed David's relationship with his girlfriend whilst trying to get Derek over his phobia. Sometimes Derek would make just about any excuse he could think of for not going out, he would use the excuse that his girl friend who lives in Leeds with a baby of theirs is such a jealous girl and afraid of him going out, in fear that he would meet someone else and really gets all in a mood when she hears that Derek's out having a good time meeting new people whilst she is stuck in doors looking after their baby. Tania, Derek's girlfriend is afraid of loosing Derek and believes that Derek will find someone else and leave her. Tania loves Derek dearly and when they both left school together four years ago Derek asked her to marry him; Tania said yes she would marry Derek, but under one condition she warned him by saying there is one rule of our engagement, and this is that she doesn't want him chatting up other women. Tania points her finger in Derek's face and reminds him by saying all right. Ever since that moment Derek has used that flimsy excuse for not going out and enjoying himself. He's out of order; I think the plain truth of the matter is that Derek

finds night clubbing and going down to the local boozer a complete and utter waste of time and a bit of a drag, and would sooner be all tucked up on the sofa at home watching something educational like Panorama' or simply playing on his home computer, but is too coward to admit it. But relentless and persistent are Derek's flat mates they simply will not give in too easily and keep badgering on at Derek. One night, Dave completely lost his rag with Derek and shouted at him; spelling out to him that that's a bull shit of an excuse, and they stopped speaking for a whole week, and you can imagine the atmosphere in the house they shared, at times, it was pretty hostile to say the least. The other two of Derek's flat mates were also beginning to feel rather unconvinced of Derek's imaginary story about having a girlfriend called Tania from Leeds who's supposed to of had a baby for Derek, so one night, Mary, one of the girls they shared the house with who Derek is not attracted to arranged a blind date for Derek in the house. Mary's mate turns out to be a complete nightmare. And the whole evening is destroyed and ends up going pear shaped, and all the more frustrating for Derek he ended up missing out on his favourite programme "Star Trek," by being polite to Mary in lending his friendship to her for the evening. Derek on the other hand was quite curious to see just how the meeting would turn out. Derek's decision on sharing the house was mainly for economical reasons and certainly was not for a boyfriend girlfriend situation; as there was no one there in particularly he really fancied. Anyway, Sally, one of the girls who shared the house with us was having her 26th birthday and was as desperate as hell to loose her virginity and who do you think her main prey was ay? Me!!!!!!!!!!!!!!!! Now, if I were to describe Sally to you, you would quite understand why I weren't interested. She looked like a female sumo wrestler, not exactly feminine type if you know what I mean. Anyway, what had happened was, she had got me pretty drunk that evening, and things started to get pretty steamy, at least from Sally point of view; she was like an animal, she was over me like a rash, and extremely desperate. She found me irresistible, and started doing all kinds of bizarre sexy moves towards me, it was awful. Meanwhile, David, Lawrence, Clifford and Lloyd were all pissed as a parrot downstairs with Barbara, Kate and Louise, the three other girls'who shared part of the house with us. Sally thought the time was perfect for the both of us to get "Mr. bombastic". Sally started coming on so strong, telling me all kinds of things like I'm a real nice guy, and how she had fancied me like rotten the moment she first laid her eyes on me, but hadn't the courage to tell me this up until now; and how this was really the first opportunity she had up until now to tell me this because now we had actually been left alone together, and even more poignant, it was her birthday. Sally really started to open up to me by telling me that she has never had a boy friend before and how men would always chat up her friends and always ignored her. She looked me straight in my eyes and said to me I know I'm not as pretty as all the other girls Derek but I feel I have a lot to offer a guy; I'll wash and iron for you Derek; I can be of use to you Derek, Sally say's. I noticed a single tear drop from her eye as she opened up her heart to me. Weeping in front of me I embraced her and consoled her the best I could when to my amazement she moved her mouth in the direction of mine; now by this stage if the truth be told I'm still a little bit tipsy; anyway, I give her a quick peck on the cheek, and then on her mouth; I knew that was what she was expecting; I could feel the adrenaline rushing, and knew before long if I did not pull back she would be all over me like a rash; it was too late, we were entangled in somewhat of a bizarre passionate embrace, and we started kissing, first gently, then ever so roughly; then gently, then ever so rough again, and by this time we were so overwhelmed by our bodily functions, we tore the house down; it was what she had been wanting for such a long time, and who better to do it with, Derek. But then, suddenly everything changed, my senses suddenly came back to me, and I hit the pillows with a bump; I realized suddenly what the implications would be, and what a messy situation I was getting myself in to; I had a child, a future wife, who was extremely jealous, and if Tania had the minutest incline that I was seeing someone else, she would go ballistic. Going clubbing was quite enough for her, having a fling, would have been absolutely hell. I poised for a moment to have a deep think, and decided almost instantly not to pursue this relationship with Sally any further, and decided to end it with immediate effect. I explained to Sally the reason why I came to this decision, and how Tania would not approve, and with that said she let go one hell of a screams!!!!!!!!!!!!!!!!!!!!!!!!! I explained to her that I can't have anything to do with her, and how it was all a terrible mistake. I also explained to Sally how we can only be friends and friends only, and how I've already got a fiancée and child, and how I love them very much, and if Tania was ever to find out I will loose everything, everything! What about me Sally replies, what about me, don't you care about me. Not in the same way Sally, not in the same way; please, understand Sally, it's Tania I love, not you, not you; Ahhhhhhh Sally shouts, Ahhhhhh! From that moment on Sally changed, it was almost as if she changed into a completely different person, she started F-ing and blinding and telling me that I'm a fuckin pig, and how all I wanted to do was to fuck her, and if I think, you're going to fuck me, then just leave me as if nothing ever happened you've got another thing coming. And said to me that she was going to tell that sweet little girl friend of mine just what a fucking little cheating little brat I really am. Oh no I gasped underneath my breath, realizing what the implications would be; and judging by the serious look on Sally's face, it told me that she really meant it, and she really would do it. So I pretended that I loved her as well, and told her, I just needed some time to work things out, I just need some time to work things out.

The following day I woke up at three o'clock in the morning; I just couldn't sleep; I kept waking up thinking to my self, what am I going to do, I had Sally, that blooming freak on my mind; and kept reminding myself of the type of problem she is likely to cause if she went and opened her big mouth. I got out of bed and walked up and down the bedroom thinking about Tania and our two-year engagement, and how everything could be all out of the window if she was ever to find out. This anxiety put an added strain on my studies, especially, whilst studying psychology, which involves intense study; I kept repeating to myself I don't need all of this, I need to pass my exams; I walked down the stairs and into the kitchen for a cup of strong black coffee, and to my surprise, I heard the kitchen door shut behind me, It was Sally, dressed in a black laced see- through negligee. She said to me, I just couldn't sleep Derek; I've been thinking about you all night; she came closer to me rubbing her boobs against me; I tried my best to resist an erection, but it was no use, and we made love again, and all over the kitchen table, and then all over the floor, and once again back in Sally's room, we end up both totally exhausted, and fell asleep. The following week I was expecting Tania round, as we had planned to spend the weekend together because we hadn't seen each other for a few months; Tania was busy looking after our baby Pete, and wasn't feeling particularly sexy, with all the breast feeding etc, and the general looking aftering of him. I guess all of that had taken its toll on her, but was all part of something she had to live with. The weekend came by ever so quickly and all what was going through my head was how I was going to disguise the fact that Sally and I had a fling. Tania, for some strange reason had a suspicion when she found whilst cleaning up in my bedroom an earring of Sally's, which she must have lost in my bedroom amongst our mad passionate moments. Sally had lost her earring under my bed. It was an unusual type of earring, it had a distinctive look to it; it was a gold Egyptian heads type of earring. That afternoon, Tania had noticed the very same earring Sally was wearing, and noticed how she was only wearing one. At first, Tania did not know how to confront either of us about this, but Tania was not the type of person to hold back on her thoughts; she liked to get to the bottom of things. That evening, to build her confidence up, Tania had got through half a bottle of Vodka and orange, and the way she felt she was ready to take on an army. She just couldn't restrain herself any longer; she had just flipped; (Tania) Yeah that's right Sally you "whore," she said, you've been sleeping with my man aven't you? I watched on, as she directed her speech across the room to Sally, and says in a slurrish tone of voice across the living room at Sally. We all just look on in shear astonishment, thinking to ourselves, what is she talking about? By this stage, we were all having a peaceful and relaxing evening in watching the rugby on television; it was the Lions versus the All Blacks (Tania). Couldn't you find yourself your own bloke instead of taking mine? Tania directs he speech over to Sally; (Sally) what are you talking about Tania, Sally replies? You know what I'm Fucking talking about you fucking whore. (Tania). Who do you think I am stupid? (Sally) I think you've probably had a wee too much to drink Tania, (Tania) that's right, I know I've bloody had too much to drink awright, and you're the reason for it, and in a flash, Tania leaped onto Sally, pulling her hair and scratching her face. Dave and I jumped in immediately and grabbed hold of Tania, and tore her away from Sally, preventing her from doing any further damage. The rage Tania was in she would have killed her. I lead Tania into the kitchen, and did my best to calm her down. Everyone else just looked on in shear and utter shock, as nobody quite understood quite what was going on. Sally made an attempt to follow us into the kitchen, but Tania just turned around and said to Sally you better just get out of my face. Two hours later and Tania cooled down. I tried to explain to Tania that she has got it all wrong, but to my horror,

Sally walks straight into the kitchen and reveals everything to Tania; it were almost as if she were in bloody court or something swearing under oath, or on the bible or something. Sally reckoned, and what's more Tania; I'm expecting his baby; I just listen to Sally in total horror, and total disbelief, that she would try to wreck our two year engagement like this, without even giving me the opportunity to explain to Tania myself. Tania screams, Ahhhhhh!!!!! And says, it's over Derek, it's over, I never want to see you again; and makes her way over to the front door saying to Sally, and you Sally, I hope you rot in hell, its people like you who causes break ups in happy family homes, and she slams the door behind her blam! And walk's off.

I WANT HALF

This is a story about a robber called Mike, who robs a jewellery shop and is pursued by an extremely angry and die hard, determined to catch him shopkeeper. Mike had been watching the jewellery shop for weeks and carefully selected exactly what he wanted to take. Mike had always wanted a Rolex watch, so he thought to himself, I'm not going to pay three grand for one, I'll nick it. Mike had only planned on taking the one Rolex watch, but realizing that he could get away with more than one, he actually ended up with six of the buggers; and Mr. Thomas the owner of the shop was certainly not going to see his hard earned investments vanish in front of his very eyes, not like that, and certainly not without a chase and a battle. Mr. Thomas was sixty five at the time, and the last time he had ran after anything, and certainly not in that fashion, ooh, must have been at least thirty years ago. Anyway, as he began chasing after Mike, he could feel his heart beginning to pump, and started to feel a little wheezy, so he backed off the chase; holding onto his chest, then falling down onto his knees; Mr. Thomas had suffered a sudden heart attack. A woman had noticed Mr.Thomas chasing after Mike, and heard him yelling stop that thief! When she heard this, she ran into the launderette and phoned the police straight away. Within minutes, you could hear the sirens from two blocks away; Mike had heard them too, and decided to run into a nearby café, some four streets away, hoping to hide away until everything had quietened down. The lady in the café had noticed Mike being out of breath; she had also heard the police sirens going. This could not have been a coincidence she thought to her self. This was not the first time Mike had used her place as some sort of hiding place; and the police had questioned Mary the café owner several time before about what type of business she was running? And Mary was beginning to get pretty cheesed off with all the agro she was getting, and not getting anything out of it. This time she was determined to get something out of it. Mary confronted Mike, saying to him, they're after you aren't they? Mike stuttered.... no Mary said to Mike, you had better tell me the truth or I'll call the police right now! Mike replies, all right then, yeah.... They are; Mary took Mike into the back room, and says to Mike, show us what you got then; Mike takes out one Rolex watch, but Mary notices a huge bulge in his pockets, and tells him show us the rest; Mike then takes out six Rolex watches each with a price tag of £8,000!!.

Mary says to Mike, look, you can stay here, it's safe, but on one condition, I want half. Mike agrees, and gives Mary three watches; Mike retreats in the shop for six hours; the time was approximately 5. o'clock, when he had done the snatch; it was also the time that Mr.Thomas normally closed up for the day. Anyway, by the time Mike decided to come out of Mary's café, it was after 11.oclock, and dark. Throughout Mikes stay in the café, all what Mike was thinking about was how he was going to do a dirty on Mary, and keep all six of his watches. Mike had noticed an empty milk bottle on the shelf, and just as Mary turned around to look out of the back window, Mike then suddenly picked up the bottle, and bolted Mary over the head!!!!!!!!!!!!!!!!!!!!!!!!!

Mary screamed AHHHHHHHHHH!!!!!!!!!!!!! And dropped to the ground, with blood pouring out all over her head, Mike panic's, and run's out of the café, grabbing the watches which Mary had left on the shelf.

Later that evening when Mike when got home, he switches on the television, and watches the 12 o'clock news, and hears of the robbery which he did, and how the shopkeeper Mr.Thomas had died of a sudden heart attack, culminating from the robbery, and how Mike was the cause of Mr. Thomas's sudden death. This incident had made the police even more determined to catch the culprit. They immediately started with their shop to shop enquiries to ascertain whether anyone had seen a scruffily dressed man with a green Adidas hat on running away from the shop; they rounded up all the information they had gathered, when finally they got around to Mary's shop, and noticed her with a bandage on her head; they asked her what had happened to her? Mary replied, oh I slipped over in the bath. They asked her whether she had noticed anything. Mary replied, as a matter of fact, there was a boy who was in here earlier who came in huffing and puffing as if he had just ran the Olympics; and yes, he was wearing a green Adidas hat; Mary gave them a full description of Mike. It wasn't long before the police were knocking on Mike's door; in fact they gave Mike a visit the very next day, because they had found Mike's fingerprints plastered all over the shelf, from where he had snatched the watches. Mike tried to deny it at first, but with the positive identification from Mary, the police had enough evidence to nail him. Sadly for Mr. Thomas though, he never lived to hear of Mike's capture, or for that matter give Mike a damn good hiding.

SHE'S STARING AT ME

We came together by pure chance; it was the summer holidays and our parents had sent us both to Southend for the day with the play school. She was eleven and I was ten; we had taken the same coach, and throughout the one and a half-hour journey, every time I looked around, I noticed this piercing gaze, from this girl who was sat behind me; at first I thought, that's bad manners; but then realized it was a stare of infatuation. It can be said, that guys are always reading into the wrong signals. Anyway, I was happy to find out later that my intuition was correct; it was a stare of infatuation; but at first I felt a little embarrassed, embarrassed, but really over-whelmed that someone had taken an interest in me.

We finally reached our destination, and everyone gave a three cheers salute, saluting, hip hip hooray, hip hip hooray, hip hip hooray, and with that said, everyone stampeded off of the bus. We all made a quick dash for the sea, to dipped our toes in, and test the temperature.

All the parents grouped up together, and all the boys rushed off in the direction of the arcade. The girls seemed to be content staying at the beach, all apart from "Cindy" she waited around for me. Striking up an instant conversation that seemed to revolve around me; she complemented me on seeming like a pretty cool guy, and how she would like to hang around with me; she said to me that the girls were all too bitchy, and how she couldn't trust them; she also explained to me how one of her best friend's had ran off with her previous boyfriend, and how she has been terribly scared to trust anyone, ever since. I thought to myself, there was someone else, someone else before me? She reassured me, that it was only a platonic relationship. Thwuu! I gasped. Cindy had long since made her mind up that she preferred to have boys as close friends, as opposed to girls. We hanged out together, spending most of the time just sat on the beach, talking about school, and how wonderful it was to have a whole six weeks off. Cindy was an only child, and I, I had come from a comparatively large family, of four. As the evening drew to an end, I realized just how wonderful a person Cindy was, and how throughout our seven hours that we had spent together, I felt at totally ease with her; it was almost as though I knew her for ages. She was an amazing person. The time was nearing towards eight o'clock, and time to mount the bus, as it had previously been arranged that the bus would depart at eight o'clock sharp. Anyway, I guess we must had totally lost all senses of the time, in our besotted state of mind of being together, we totally lost track of the time. We arrived back at the car park fifteen minutes later than previously arranged, and the bus hadn't wasted any time in departing; and what had happened was, the bus had traveled half the way back into London, when one of my mates, Tony, asked where's Derek? Tony shouted! Where's Derek!!!!!! Driver stop! Derek's not on the bus. The driver slams down on the brakes, breaking to a halt!!!!! And onto the lay–by. "Shit", he said. The four parents that were on the bus looked on at the children in utter disgust, it was almost as though we were all to blame. The driver sat there fuming, huffing and puffing all the way back to Southend. He took the nearest roundabout we came to and made his way back to Southend. By this time, it was getting dark, and the bus was scheduled back by 9.30pm. But, by the time we had picked up Derek and Cindy, who was only too pleased to see that the bus had come back for them, as they had no real hope in getting back, and hardly had any money on them, they probably would have had to hitched hike a lift back or something.

But anyway, as we pulled up in the coach station, I noticed the looked on their faces, it was a look of despair; they looked like a pair of lost sheep; they were only too happy to see that we had returned to collect them. The driver however was not so embracing, and welcomed them with one hell of a blast of a shout. Yelling, you stupid idiots!!!!!!!!!!!!!!!!!!!!!!!!!!!!!!

This is a tragic story about a boy called Jim (nick name) "Jim bob," who lived for love but never received it; and the only way he knew he would get any attention was to take his own life. Jim bob, was a solitary type of person who wanted only one thing out of life, and that was to be loved and have a girlfriend; he needed someone who would adore him, and love him; a love that he longed for, but never received. All the girls that Jim bob would see and have desires for, for some reason, he would not know how to approach them; he never had the confidence to speak to them. On occasions, Jim Bob would force his self to pluck up the courage, and when he did, what would often happen, they would make him look like a fool, by taking the mickey out of the way Jim Bob would stutter. This reaction could only diminish Jim Bob's confidence further still. Later, this affect would prove to be catastrophic. He never ever received the reception he'd hoped for; the affect had taken its toll on him, leaving Jim bob, often feeling perplexed and confused; he often felt frustrated and unwanted, and somewhat insignificant in life; it was almost as if life it self had no meaning with out love, and Jim Bob, simply could not come to terms with his rejection. Anyway it was June the 13th 1969, and it was Jim bobs birthday, he was twenty-two years of age, and despite the telling signs of Jim Bob being rather reserved and reclusive, he would however feel more at ease being declined from society, than having to face up to embarrassing situations. Jim Bob's brother Chuck knew of his situation, but Chuck had his own problems to deal with. Chuck would often wonder to himself, where the devil is he? If he hadn't seen him for sometime; because the one place where Jim bob would visit was the family home; but ever since Jim Bob started to feel terribly self conscious, the word elusiveness would be kind of an understatement; Jim bob could hardly be seen for dust.

Anyway, what had happened was, we were expecting Jim bob to come home to celebrate his 22nd birthday with the family as he promised, it was 8pm, and Jim bob still hadn't arrived; it was a Sunday, and he said he would be there by 5, so mother said to me, why don't you go around and call him? As Jim bob only lived a stone throw away from the family home, I decided to make a quick trip over there; I rang the bell dring dring, dring dring, dring dring. No answer? So I thought to myself, let me check at the back, he must be at the back, so I walked through the side path at the side of the house, and shouted, Jim bob!!!!!!!!! You there; Still no answer, at this point I was beginning to get a little worried, because Jim bob rarely ventured out, I looked through the window, and spotted, Jim bob, slumped over his chair, with his hands laid flat out on the table, I screamed,……. Jim bob Jim bob had taken an overdose and killed himself; I guess, he must have said to himself, I can't cope with this anymore.

YOU'RE NICKED!

This is a story about a boy called Joe, who found himself a job working in a chocolate factory. Joe loved chocolate bars ever so much, that he decided to nick a lorry load of them, and try to sell them two hundred miles away from where he lived. Joe watched and waited for the right moment to come along, before he made his move. He noticed how the security guard (Harry) drank loads of coffee to keep him awake throughout the night. Anyway, the story goes that Joe got talking to Harry, and started asking him indirect questions about their security. Joe thought to himself, Harry wouldn't suspect anything. Joe always wondered to himself, why they put a dopey old goat as head of security; with a big responsibility of looking after thousands of pounds worth of chocolate bars, which were all loaded in lorry's, parked in the loading bay? Joe thought to himself, all I've got to do is to find an excuse to have to chat to Harry, perhaps, striking up a conversation about what football team he support's, and make him feel comfortable with me, you know what I mean, to the point where he'll even offer make me a cup of tea or coffee, then whilst he's not looking, put a sleeping pill in his coffee, and when I see him just about to nod off, tell him that I'd better be off now. Then, hide in the toilets and waits until the dopey goat doses off to sleep. I'm sure it wouldn't take him long, because I've had to wake him up several times before whilst he was on his shift. It wasn't long before the pill had taken effect, and Harry was sleeping like a baby. (Harry), (Harry) Joe called? No answer, and just to make sure that he was well out, Joe slapped him around the face, then grabs hold of the keys, which was hanging on the wall, and makes his way over to the lorry, which is packed with Mars bars galore; Joe starts up the lorry, and drives it out of the yard; unknown to Joe, the lorry is fitted with a tracking devise system. Joe heads straight for the M1 motorway, and heads two hundred miles away to (Leeds), thinking to him self, no one will get me up ere; and parks the lorry down some side road, hoping that, come the morning, he'll go out and sell them to every Tom Dick and Harry newsagent there are in the district. Meanwhile, back at the factory, the drug is wearing off of Harry, and he wakes up at 4.30am in the morning, only to realize that the lorry he was meant to be looking after, the big 30 footer, had disappeared. It was almost as if it had done a "Houdini." Harry gets on the "dog and bone" straight away to the police, they track it down to the exact spot where "Joe" was hiding out, down some side street, and to Joe's horror, he's woken up by the Leeds Police Authority, with one hell of a blaze of a shout, yelling your Nicked!!!!!!!!!!!!!!!!

I'LL KILL HER

This is a story about twins who are separated at birth and sent to foster parents for economical reasons. Both of the twins are deaf and dumb and could be quite a hand full to handle at times. As time went on their behavior pattern became more and more irritable, especially to the male foster parent Mr. Powell. At times he would lose his temper and lash out, sometimes, injuring the twin sister (Jane). It wasn't long before Mr. Powell soon started drinking. Well, after a few months of living with Jane, I guess the stress had taken its toll; and one day, Mr. Powell just flipped and turned onto Jane for drinking his alcohol. Jane had managed to get through a whole bottle of scotch whilst Mr. Powell was out with his friends. Anyway, what had happened was, that day Mr. Powell had returned home after a day out with his friends only to realize that Jane had gotten through a whole bottle of his Whisky, and Mr. Powell was furious!!!!! And what had made it worse; Jane was legless and muttering a whole load of nonsense to him. And in a rage, Mr. Powell grabbed Jane by her neck and started strangling her; not intentionally to kill her, and completely unaware that the Jane was already quite dehydrated from the alcohol; Jane slowly drifted away…. Mr. Powell had held Jane in an ever so tight grip around her throat that she simply just collapsed in his hands. He had killed her. He then started thinking to himself where am I going to dispose of this body? Mary, his wife was soon expected back from her holiday in the South of France. So he temporarily hid her in the cellar; but was not happy with her being there, so he moved her into the shed at the back of the garden where he kept all his tools. He knew his wife Mary seldomly ventured out there, as she had no real reason for going in there; but for some strange reason, whilst Mary was hanging her washing out on the line, she smelt a horrible smell coming from the shed, so she creped up to the shed to find out what it was that was smelling so badly; she opened the shed door, and unruffled all the hay, and to her horror, she saw Jane's body. She screamed!!!! And ran back into the house and asked Mr. Powell what had happened? Mr. Powell replied, calm down woman, calm down. But Mary, his wife, was so horrified with what she had seen because she had never seen a dead body before. She kept asking him, what happened; what happened? Mr. Powell relented, and slowly explained to Mary how things had got a little out of hand. Mary was a loyal wife to Mr. Powell; and whatever had happened, she was always going to stick by him; she even started to suggest how they should dispose of the body, because Mary was worried sick about the smell, and didn't want her neighbours to smell anything. So they decided to bury the body at the back of the garden, and report her missing to the police. Two weeks went by and the social services were beginning to get worried about Jane's whereabouts, because an appointment had been booked for her, which she failed to attend. Social worker Tom, who only lived a few hundred yards away decided he would just pop around to the Powell's house to check.

Mr. Powell answered the door and Tom explained how Jane hadn't kept her appointment, and how he was just checking up on her. Mr. Powell explained to Tom that how Jane had been missing for two weeks; and how he'd reported her to the police, but hadn't heard a word. The neighbours were also beginning to get a little suspicious, because they would often see Jane playing in the back garden. The social services immediately started their own investigation and went around to Jane's sisters' house Sarah to find out whether she had gone around there; but that turned out to be a negative. Sarah, Jane's twin sister happened to be possessed with extreme talent, and a gift with psychic and telepathic powers; she had also helped the police several times in the past to solve some of their most complicated cases; and had been visioning at the time just what Mr. Powell had done to her sister. She saw it all in her vision; Jane had built up a highly respected reputation for herself with the police; but when she tried to explaining to her carer, just what she was seeing, her carer (Isobel), was rather dismissive about it all, and completely refused to accept any of it, claiming that it was all a load of rubbish. Nonsense she said. Meanwhile the police had been carrying out their investigation and Sarah had gone to the police, and led them to where her sister's body was. The police had followed her to the Powell's accommodation and was quite taken up by this, as they had not too long ago been there. And just as Sarah is about to approached the house she started crying and screaming, pointing in the direction of the side door leading to the back garden of the house. The police took the hatch off the door and made their way into the back garden. At this point the police had confronted and cautioned Mr. Powell and told him that he was not obliged to say anything, and that anything he says would be taken down and used in evidence against him. The police man officer Dibble reaches for one of Mr. Powell's spades from out of his shed and starts to dig, and after about a foot of excavating into the earth they notice a hand appear, followed by the rest of the body. Sarah was so angry, and started kicking and punching Mr. Powell. The police officer had to restrain her from her anger. They arrested Mr. Powell and charged him. He was found guilty and sentenced to life in prison.

Knock knock, the door sounded, I knew it was her because she never came around during the day. I always wondered why she would not visit me during the day; I was always lonely during the days, and in great need of companionship. Anyway, she knocked and I answered, “Mary” is that you? Yes Derek, it’s only me, open the door. I opened the door, and she threw her body into mine, almost as though I was her saviour. I would be always waiting impatiently whilst Mary was away.
How was your day today Mary I asked? Oh, pretty much the same as yesterday, only I had this punter who refused to pay me, and when I refused to give him a free blowjob, he went completely berserk!! He treated me as though I were some trash or something. Anyway, I refused to give him what he wanted, and he left; honestly, the time I spent with him, I could have earn myself £20 quid, dick head Mary moaned, wrapping her arms around me. Anyway, how was your day Derek? Oh, pretty boring Mary; all I did was fit a shelve in the bathroom, that was about it, and made myself several cups of tea, and just crashed out on the sofa, watching Home and Away. To tell the truth Mary, I wish you were here with me; instead of being out there working. (Mary) Derek, lets not get into that argument again Derek, you know someone has to go out and earn the bread, or else we’ll be out on the street. (Derek) Oh, but Mary I miss you like crazy, and I just wish you could be here with me. (Mary) don’t worry Derek; just another twelve months of this, and I figured out we would have enough money for a decent deposit to put down on a house, instead of renting this crummy old bed-sit, and life would be much better ay Derek, what do you say? Derek replies reservedly, and in an uncertain manner; ….yeah, I guess so Mary. I guess so.
The following evening, the time was approximately 12.05am, and Mary hadn’t arrived yet, and by this time Derek was beginning to tap away at his fingers like crazy,

wondering where the devil is she. He was worried sick that something dreadful might have happened to her, as she was normally always prompt. The time was fast approaching 12.45, and Mary still hadn't arrived. Where is she? Derek kept asking himself; always thinking of the worse possible scenario, of something dreadfully happening to her, Derek was worried sick. Three hours later still no sign of Mary. That morning, Mary strolled in around 5 o'clock. Anyway, she knocked the door; Mary is that you? Yes Derek; open up. Where were you, I was worried sick; where have you been for heavens sake? Mary replied, I met someone Derek, yes I met someone, and he's a millionaire; and I'm leaving you.

It all started off whilst I was in the Flower Pot Hotel having lunch; I realized whilst watching the national lottery on T.V that I was one number short of winning the jackpot; feeling disgusted about not winning, I screwed up the ticket and threw it in the bin; I was totally gutted for having missed out on such a fortune of £6,000,000, and having to settle for a measly £40 quid for the numbers I had, it hardly seemed worth collecting, so I just threw away the tickets in disgust. I remember throwing it in the bin, and walking out of the Flowerpot. On my way home, I start thinking to myself, if I played the same ticket number again, I might win next time? The following day, I returned to the flowerpot, because this was where I had my regular lunch. I explained to Joey the cleaner how sick I felt about me missing out on a fortune; I also recall explaining to him how I couldn't be bothered to claim the lousy £40 quid, and told him if he finds the ticket amongst the rubbish, he can have it. I'm not sure whether Joey went ravishing through the bins looking for my ticket or not, I wasn't particularly bothered either, until I reached home, and whilst relaxing on the sofa, I heard on the news, how's there's a 99 point 9% of a chance of the same numbers coming up the following week end; apparently it had happened once before; this really did get me thinking. The irony was that, the same newsreader, "Bill Murray," proclaimed something similar on "April fools" day, to increase sales and nothing happened, but, I still had a hunch. Anyway, I rush back to the Flower Pot; I spot Joey doing his cleaning, I demanded Joey to let me make a note of the numbers; Joey also happens too hears the news and absolutely refuses to give me the numbers. At first I think he thinks I'm going to take back the ticket, and refuse to let me see it, so I try another strategy telling him that he can keep the £40 quid, all I want is the numbers, but then Joey denies even having the ticket, so I go on the search looking for my elusive ticket. I check with the other cleaners, they all reply, they haven't seen it. I asked "Jack" one of the concierge staff, and he says to me wait a minute, Mr. Russell picked something up from out of the bin, yeah that's right, I noticed Mr. Russell ravishing through the bins, and picking something out of there; I thought to myself, it looked rather peculiar and rather odd of him to be ravishing though the bins in that manner; he must have overheard you when you screamed, and heard what you said to Joey. So, I rush through the dining room, bouncing past the guests whilst they're having their lunch, bounced past one of the waiters, knocking the soup all over his uniform, and scantically made my way through the corridor. I spot one of the residents, and asked her if she knew where Mr. Russell's room was, she pointed me in the direction of where Mr. Russell's room is, and without any hesitation what so ever at all, I rush straight into Mr. Russell's room; Mr. Russell seemed somewhat astounded and shocked, and had somewhat of a look of dismay, that someone could just come barging in his room like that, and he shouted what the hell do you want! I explained to Mr. Russell that I don't want any trouble all right; all I want is my ticket back; I know you picked it up, because Jack, the concierge spotted you; Mr. Russell mutters, …what are you talking about; and says to me, you bust into my room without even knocking the door, and claim that I've got your ticket! Are you mad, or are you insane, get out of here before I call the police; I'm not moving I said to Mr. Russell, until I get my ticket. Mr. Russell relents, and says to me all right you can have it. And unknown to me, that slimey little slime ball Mr. Russell, had something up his sleeves. He lies back on his bed, and says to me; just throw me that jacket over there, the tickets in my pocket. I throw him his jacket, and then suddenly, Mr. Russell pulls out a small revolver from underneath his pillow.

I notice the revolver, and dashed the jacket in his face, kicking the revolver out of his hand; I quickly pick up the revolver, and looked at Mr. Russell in utter disgust. Mr.

Russell replies, well you know, you can't take any chances in this business, there's all sorts of weirdoes hanging around the place. I take the jacket, and the revolver, and run off. I took the bullets out of Mr. Russell' gun, and returned it to him two days later, just in case he tried to pull a fast one. It's the day of the lottery; and I watch on impatiently, as all my numbers come up, just as predicted, and I win a staggering £2,000,000. I bank the cheque, and book myself a first class trip to the Bahamas. Whereby I lie on the beach drinking Pina Colado's all day. Life could not have been better.

Todd, Jerry, Sam and I had decided we wanted to get out of England for a bit, because we were all pretty cheesed off with the repetitiveness of the hustle and bustle of urban living; to tell the truth we were all completely bored stiff. We all agreed that the repetitiveness of our work schedules was beginning to have an affect on our lives and we were all feeling slightly discontented with life; we were all single and neither of us had any real commitments or responsibilities, so we decided to go over to Holland. On our arrival, we stacked all our gear at the hotel, and walked around the local supermarkets to get a feel of the place; walking around in a different country felt so much different from where we had come from, it was like a breath of fresh air, the people seemed to be more relaxed, and I asked Todd how he was feeling being away from London? He replied it's a change well deserved ay…. On the third day of our stay, we decided we wanted to go and try to meet some girls, so we headed up town, had a snack at one of the restaurants, then found a club called "Changes" I thought to myself at the time, that's a funny name for a club, but never really gave it a second thought after that. Anyway, we arrived at the club around eleven o'clock, and were amongst the first set of people to arrive, and by the time it was around about 1.30am, more people started to arrive at the club. I spotted four leggy blondes enter in and make there way over to the bar; one of them was looking at me straight in the eye; Todd reckoned to me what do you think about that lot Derek? I reckoned to Todd looks good to me; so Todd and I made our way over to them; Jerry and Sam followed later; I could tell that they were interested by the way they were smiling at us, and giving us the come on. So I put my groovy walk on, and walked over to them. I picked the blond with the longest legs, and Todd picked the brunette. We got talking, and things were going great! I figured out, we'd scored. As the night went on, we decided to take to the dance floor; my one was a great dancer; we danced the whole night through until the early hours of the morning. I guess it must of been 5 o'clock; when I looked around, only to notice that Todd, Jerry and Sam, and the four bird's we were with, were just about the only one's left in the club, so we decided it was time to go. Kate, the bird that I was with, asked me if I would like to take her home; the rest of the boy's, all seemed as though they had scored; I thought to myself things were too good to be true, when Kate told me that they all shared the same house together; brilliant I thought, we can all be together. We got a taxi, and made our way to their house. On our arrival, the girl's made absolutely no bones about each of us going immediately to their own separate bedrooms; well, at 6.o'clock in the morning you don't really feel like chatting or playing Snakes and Ladders do you? Anyway, I went up the stairs to Kate's bedroom, and she told me that I should get undressed first; and that she would join me in a mo. She said to me that, she's just got to powder her nose; I thought to myself, yeah, right you horny bitch. Anyway, I took my clothes off and tucked into the sheet's; she appeared five minutes later, god knows what she was doing in there? But anyway, she turned the lights off, and gently slipped under the covers. Half way through the night, I heard one hell of a scream!!!!!!!!!!!!!! From Todd's room; and thought to myself the randy bastards they're at it? Then I heard footsteps tumbling down the stairs; I must admit, it didn't bother me at the time, because by this time, Kate and I were kissing and cuddling and doing fore play; and after about ten minutes of it, I could not resist putting my hands on Kate's genitals, but she moved my hands away quickly before I had a chance to touch them. We continued to kiss, and I couldn't help resisting grabbing hold of her crutch; I eventually grabbed hold of it, only to find out that what I had grabbed hold of was a pair of "bollox" I screamed!!!!!!!!!!!!!!!!!!!And immediately grabbed my trousers, and ran out!!!!!!!!!!!!!!!!!!!!!!!!!!!! I met up with the lads later that day, and they all told me that they had experienced the same thing. I said to myself never again, never again man, next time, I'm going to check out my girl properly man…..

SUNDAY MASS

Sunday morning and the dreaded thought of my mother yelling from the top of the stairs Derek! You ready! And dragging me off to church terrorized my state of well being. Anyway, that was exactly what happened. I started to put on my clothes as slowly as I possibly could in the hope that she would give up on me and say you're too late! Did she ek! She grabbed me by the scruff of my neck and frog marched me down the stairs and said brush your hair quickly, and put on your shoes we're late. We got to the church, and half way through the mass the vicar started singing, and everyone else joined in; I don't want to sing I screamed in my head!! Ten minutes later, some geezer comes round with a basket ponsing money; leave me alone I screamed again!! Fifteen minutes later, it was time to accept the bread offerings; now, having being rushed out of my house at ten o'clock first thing on a Sunday morning, I though to myself the least the vicar could have done was to offer me a decent slice of bread instead of that silly little wafer thin slice he was offering, that was hardly going to fill me up was it; and the wine, I don't want to be drinking from a glass that two hundred other people has taken a sip from before me. Mum seemed to be enjoying herself in the midst of all the singing and the kneeling. I dreaded to tell her that I was bored too tears, without getting a clip around the ear, yelling don't be stupid it's great! Finally, the mass had ended, and it was time to go home. What a relief I thought. I felt like bolting out of there like some raving lunatic shouting hooray! Now, that really would have put the shiver up their spines. By the time I stood up to leave, I had cramp from all of that sitting, kneeling lark; it was getting on my ruddy nerves. Anyway, we got outside, and it was ten degrees below freezing, and mother had spotted one of her friends, and believe it or not she started nattering away!!! I screamed in my head, I wanna go home, I wanna go home……..

MISTAKEN IDENTITY

I was completely shocked to stumble over two grown up men deliberating between themselves, as to which one of them was going to steal this poor old man's briefcase that I noticed slumped across the seat of his Jaguar Daimler car. He was obviously too tired to drive, and it seemed to me like he probably took a brief nap, then fell into a deep sleep. He was hanging rather precariously with one arm leaning out of his wide opened window; he also seemed as though perhaps, I'm not certain, but, maybe, he may have had one too many to drink, and was trying his best to wear it off. When suddenly I noticed the mugger lean towards the window of the man's car and snatched the man's briefcase and leg it down the road!!!! The man must have felt something, and was doing his best to kick himself out of his sleep; and after a few attempts, he managed to wake himself up, only to notice the thief legging it down the road; and if for some strange reason, despite seeing the thief running off with his briefcase, it would appear as if he suspected me as his main suspect. At this point I started thinking to myself oh my god, oh my god, what if he thinks it's me, and that I had something to do with it. Panicking, I ran away; and ironically in the same direction as the mugger; it was a bit bizarre really; but at the time, all I was thinking of, was that I wanted to make myself as scarce as possible, and wanted absolutely nothing to do with it, nothing whatsoever. I heard the man shout stop! This was all the more worrying for me, because by this time, the mugger was about fifty yards away, and the man in the car seemed convinced that he wanted me..... I heard him start his car up, and quickly do a three-point turn, and came racing towards the both of us, bloody hell I was thinking to myself. I saw the mugger jump over a fence and make his way across a field that was completely out of reach for a car. I tried pointing my hand in the direction of which way the thief had gone, but he seemed so pig-headed ignorant, he was determined to get me. I tried my very best to loose him, but I guess I must have ran out of road, because not knowing where I was heading, I ran down a cul de sac. The man cornered me, jumped out of his car, and lunged at my throat like a maniac. He stood over me, gazing at me, with wide puffing steel blue eyes; his face was as red as a beetroot, fuming with rage; and I thought to myself, this guy is going to rip my bloody head off!!! I tried my best to explain that it wasn't me who took his briefcase, but it seemed, despite him noticing me not having anything on me; he still weren't having any of it. I'm guessing, but I reckon he thought I had hidden it somewhere. Now he said, I'm going to give you one a last chance to give it back; I murmured, horrified that I hadn't anything to do with it, when to my astonishment and horror, I felt one hell of a wallop across my face!!! My head was spinning in a daze; now give it back I heard him say. By this time, we were causing a bit of a commotion and were beginning to draw attention towards ourselves from people watching through their windows. Then suddenly I heard a window open and heard someone shout out, do you want me to call the police? Yes, call the police the man replied; oh leave it out guv I replied; I told you, I've got nothing to do with it; the guy you want, jumped over the fence, and made his way off that way, as I pointed in the direction where I saw the thief had run. It seemed as though we were arguing for hours, when suddenly I heard, Der Der, Der Der,Der Der, Der Der. Then suddenly, I saw two young police men jump out of their car, and before I could utter a blinking word, they slapped a pair of handcuffs on me and whisked me away to the nearby old bill shop, I was livid!!!!!!!!!

MUGGER HARRIS

This is a story about an intelligent boy who got involved with the wrong crowd, who stole, took drugs and always ended up in fights and arguments with rival gangs. These fights would normally be for owing money to their suppliers, or if another member of gang tried to get off with one of another member of gangs girls or something. Anyway, Harris would often try his best to avoid confrontations, but would always get caught up in the frackard, because of his so-called best mates' fiery temper. Micky, Harris's so called best mate, once got involved in a heated row with one of his rivals for selling some drugs to one of his customers'; and Micky 's rival Tommy was not best pleased with Harris, even though it was actually Micky that sold the stuff to Tommy's customer, Joey. I actually think Micky did this to wind up Tommy. Anyway, the story has it that Tommy went around to Harris's house because he didn't know where Micky lived and started showering Harris with a stream of abuse, calling him just about every name under the sun. Harris stood at the top floor window of his flat trading names back, and it came to a point when the language started to become more and more personal especially from Tommy; Tommy started to call Harris's mother names I would not like to repeat, and when Harris heard this he totally flipped and flew down the stairs lunging a kung fu kick at Tommy, Knocking him over to the ground, he started kicking him and slapping him. A neighbour heard the commotion and was trying his best to pull them apart; at this stage Tommy was still haling abuse at Harris, and being a little worse for wear, started shouting, telling Harris that I'm going to brock you up. What had happened was, Harris's supplier just happened to be the same supplier as Tommy's and because Micky was still owing his supplier money, he was reluctant to give

Tommy any more supply, this made Tommy furious with Micky for not paying up on time; and to add insult to injury Micky had the cheek to sell some stuff to one of Tommy's customers, it infuriated him madly. When Micky heard of Harris's ten-minute bust up with Tommy, he thought to himself how am I going to get the two grand he owed to his supplier Jack, to get him self back in credit. He knew he had to get the money by the end of the week because Jack had given him a final warning. So out of despair Micky and Harris took to the streets, and naturally their main prey just happened to be soft targets, and unfortunately, that happened to be this little old lady. Having to face up to pier pressure from Micky, they both took to the streets. The time was around 10.30pm and Micky spotted a lone pensioner clutching her bag; I think she must have been coming back from the bingo or something, and Micky thought to himself yes! He said to Harris, I'll look out and you lick it. Harris crept up from behind the little old lady; the lady notices Harris's advances and scared to death, the little old lady starts to walk quicker!!!!, Harris notices this, and chases after her, and took one hell of a swipe at her bag. The woman held on to her bag ever so tightly; determined as hell not to let him get away with it, but Harris too was determined and the fight was on. Harris was so determined he ripped the bag clean off the handles, and unfortunately in Harris's determination he rips the poor old lady's finger off. Harris had torn the poor old lady's finger clean out of the socket; the woman screamed aah!!!!!!!!!!!! And Harris disappears off into the dark completely oblivious to the damage he caused to the poor little old lady. The following morning he turns the television on, only to hear of the ordeal that the victim had suffered. Fortunately, as Harris searched the full contents of the bag, he notices the finger in there. The reporter reporting the mugging made an appeal that if the mugger is listening please would he send the finger to their office so at least the woman would have a chance of saving her finger. Harris was so traumatized by his rational move, and places the finger in a parcel, with a sincere letter of apology saying that I hope you can find in your heart of heart's to forgive me. The following afternoon, Harris thought to himself, I really don't need this shit? There must be another way of making a living, and he books his self an appointment to see a rehabilitation counselor, and openly admits his drug and relationship problem's; he also explains to Mr. Charles his counselor about the people he's involved with. Mr. Charles's advise to Harris by saying to him, the first thing you need to do is to get out of the circle you're in, and secondly, go back to college, and get yourself a skill or a trade, you'll be much better off. Harris say's to Mr. Charles, I'd like to do that sir, I really would; Harris gets himself qualified as an electrician, and changes his set of so called friends, and he never looked back.

OPERATION UNTIDY

It started off with what should have been a simple operation of removing my daughter Pam's appendix. So, what I did, I made an appointment with the doctor and booked her in to the clinic; and to my horror on my arrival at the clinic I found out that all operation's was being carried out by "trainee surgeons." I was a little dubious at first, but after confronting the head surgeon, he assured me not to worry he said, it's all in safe hands he reckons? Just the thought of the "trainees" alone made me feel uncomfortable; I mean, they hardly looked over the age of seventeen; it was slightly disconcerting to say the least; considering, Pam herself was only fifteen, and they I guess could have only been a couple of years older than her at best. Anyway, it was soon Pam's turn to be treated because the girl who was sitting next to us had just gone in, and had come out in somewhat of a crouching position and holding on to her stomach, obvious in pain. I asked the receptionist what's the matter with her? She replied, oh that's a normal reaction to have a little cramp after an operation!!! It's normal, just take a seat and relax, Pam will be out before you can say "Jack Robinson" (Jack Robinson). Anyway, they called Pam, and she went in. I followed behind her, and was abruptly stopped at the operation room by would you believe it, this "junior trainee" trying to stamp his authority down, saying sorry sir, patients only. I mean, who the bloody hell does he think he is ay? But I said I'm her father; sorry sir he replied, shutting the door in my face, patience only. So I went back to my seat anxious as hell. Half an hour later, I heard one hell of a scream!!!!! It was Pam. I leaped out of my seat and rushed straight over to the operating room, to find out what was happening; I tried looking through the windows but it was no use the windows were blacked out, blurring my vision. What had happened was the blithering idiot didn't give Pam enough anesthetics, and she had woken up during the operation!! And worse still, he cut her in the wrong place, and had caused her to bleed profusely. The pain that I heard Pam was in was unbearable; and despite the doors being locked, I had to get in there. It was almost as if they were trying to kill her in there; so, I took five steps backwards, and lunged at the door, unleashing an almighty "kung fu" style kick at the door, busting it down instantly. I entered the room and said what's the bloody hell's going on in here ay? Then suddenly, I noticed three of the surgeon's who were operating on Pam suddenly spin around in shock, and had all come towards me; they held me down, and was restraining me whilst the receptionist who had heard the commotion pressed her panic alarm button alerting the security guards that there was trouble. And in a matter of seconds, along came running towards the operating room where I was in six hefty looking security guards who nailed me down to the ground and carried me away to a secure locked up unit. They placed me into their secure unit and came back an hour later to let me know how Pam's progress was getting on. Anyway, quite contrary to their initial claim that the operation would have been as smooth as a nut, and would only take around half an hour, Pam ended up spending the best part of a month in that blooming hospital after that operation; and when she was finally released she was never quite the same, always feeling sick; eventually I found a specialist who diagnosed exactly what the problem was; he knew exactly why Pam was feeling so ill, and prescribed her a dose of anti bio tic's which gradually improved Pam's condition, and eventually she started to make some improvements.

THE DAY I WON THE POOLS

I'd been working at the garage for ten years, and every day covered in oil, and often working in the rain, sometimes right up until the late hours of the night; I'd also been going through a bit a tough patch lately, trying to make ends meet paying the bills etc. They came in one after the other; it was driving me crazy. Not to mention the other big headache, the £95,000 mortgage Sally and I had taken out on the house. The pressure was quite intense to say the least; and add to the fact that we had just had our first child Zoë, who screamed her head off all day and all night; we had no alternative but to have a baby sitter come in and look after her. It was either that or Sally literally would have gone in sane. Sally also had to keep her job to help pay for some of the domestics like nappies, food etc. She held on to her job at the local supermarket where she worked as a check out girl. We always talked to one another about what it would be like if we were to win the pools, but always laughed it off, as we knew that the chance's of it coming true was one in a million. Things started to get even harder when a garage opened up a few doors away from me, undercutting my price of a service by would you believe it a whopping 50%, I'm sure it was a deliberate ploy to get rid of me? As the months went by, noticeable differences became quite apparent in my accounts. I was down by up to 75%. I was actually beginning to think that I was working for nothing; the pressures from work naturally made its way back to the home, it was terrible, because Sally and I argued for the minuteness of things, things that under normal circumstances we perhaps would have laughed at. Things got so that bad that we decided to temporarily separate. I was devastated, because I loved Sally so much. Being alone in the house was horrible; I knew I had to channel my thoughts and interests into something, or I'd go completely bananas, and the one thing that was always niggling me was money, and how I was going to settle my debts which was a complete and utter pain in the arse. So I started playing the pools; I'd been playing it for three months and by this time Sally and I had settled our differences and were living back together again. When one night I just could not get to sleep. Sally kept asking me what's wrong Derek, what's wrong? I replied, I don't know Sally; something's on my mind, but I just can't quite figure it out. It was about 5.oclock in the morning when I woke up in a rage of excitement saying I've won, I've won. Sally thought I was going off of my rocker. Anyway, I settled down, but just couldn't understand where this excitement was coming from. The posts man came bright and early that morning and delivered a pools envelope, I opened it, and it said I had won £200,000! Yes, £200,000. I was absolutely ecstatic; I just could not believe my luck. My dream had come true; it was as though God was telling me, I've suffered enough and needed a break. Sally and I just couldn't believe it, and headed straight through to the kitchen, and started dancing around the kitchen table. We were so happy. Then suddenly, as we were dancing around the kitchen table celebrating, the phone rang, dring dring! dring dring! dring dring; we weren't going to answer it at first; we were so happy and did not want to be disturbed by anyone; but it kept on ringing and ringing, so Sally relented and answered it; it was the receptionist at Littlewoods, confirming that we had won, and that we had to go to the Grosvenor Park Hotel to collect our cheque. We were so happy. Ten minutes later the phone started ringing again; dring dring, dring dring, what now for heavens sake we thought? Have they made a mistake? It was Sally's sister telling her that her beloved mother had tripped over her shoelace and had fell down three flights of stairs in the house and died. We were .....Devastated. Totally Devastated. Why? We kept asking ourselves, why? I tried to console Sally, but she was so confused and muddled up she had changed; she wouldn't have me anywhere near her; I was so baffled, I did not know quite what to do? Was I to blame in any way? Was Sally thinking to herself that if she had only stayed with her mother instead of coming back to me this would never have happened? I just don't know, but one thing for sure was she would not have me anywhere near her. I was devastated. I just couldn't think straight; and as far as the money was concerned, it was the last thing I wanted to think about at the time. I was totally confused; the woman I loved and thought I had a future with seemed to be all out of the window; she started treating me as though I were to blame for her mothers' death, and for that reason I should be rejected and treated insignificantly, it was as though our fifteen year marriage had all been futile. Sally had gone to live in the family home with her sister June, and every time I rang her, her sister would answer the phone, only to tell me that Sally doesn't want anything to do with you. Three months went by and I had gone into a form of depression and hadn't collected the cheque; then one day I said to myself, to hell with it, I might as well collect it, when a Littlewoods letter arrived in the post saying that I was too late in collecting it and that it had gone to good causes. I was doubly gutted.

THE BIG RACE

Soon after leaving school at the age of eighteen, Jerry and I had both joined Shifters Athletic club; we both trained extremely hard together and had won a lot of races. I won the majority of times and would beat Jerry by a yard or two; however, he did manage to beat me once, and he cherished that one victory like the bark to a tree; he would always remind me of that one off victory, and I'm sure, even on that occasion, he took off before the gun had actually gone off. By this time, we had been at the club for about three years and the coaches were beginning to take serious interest in the one's who were winning, like Jerry and myself. Both Jerry and I knew it was nearing the time for serious business because Alex our coach had a word with us about signing someone up soon, but he didn't say whom; however, he did say, that he only wanted the best; and from that moment on I noticed a sudden change in Jerry's behavior. I knew Jerry's girlfriend Sue had left him, so I knew he wasn't 100% up to scratch neither physically or emotionally, but there was something other than that which I could not quite get to grips with. Jerry had become rather aloof from me and would not knock for me as he normally did. But who would have thought that behind my back, Jerry was taking "Steroids" to boost his performance, so that he would beat me in the important races, so that he and not me would have been the one to be selected and signed and receive a huge cheque, leaving me in the doldrums, ay, oo? I also noticed Jerry's arms and thighs had increased enormously in size, and were looking rather like tree trunks; I remember always making sarcastic jokes at him saying to him I think you've entered the wrong competition Jerry, body building is next door; but then I thought again to myself its got to be some form of depression or something that's causing Jerry to over eat. I was wrong, I was wrong. I was wrong. I also noticed that Jerry had started hanging around with a runner called Lawrence. Perhaps, I thought to myself, he probably thinks I'm boring and Lawrence is more interesting than me; I dunno. I also noticed that whenever I happen to pass Jerry in training he would always stare at me in a strange way. Well, looking back at it, it all stands to reason, it all makes sense to me now, he knew what he was doing was wrong, and was too embarrassed to tell me that he was cheating. I guess he was fed up with me beating him all the time and knew he couldn't beat me under normal circumstances and the only way he was going to beat me was by taking those ridiculous pills. He was even prepared to gamble with his health. I guess, doing that to himself must have seemed easier for Jerry to cope with than accepting that I was the better man. Anyway, it was the big day, yes the big day. It was selection time, and the day of the semi finals; there were eight of us in the race, and as we walked up to the track, I noticed Jerry hadn't even looked at me. We all got into position; Jerry was three lanes away from me, the referee said, on the marks, get set, bang! The gun went off. Jerry took off like a bat out off hell!!!! He was like a bullet, like the bionic man. He left the lot of us standing; he was incredible, you should have seen him; and by the time Jerry had finished the one hundred meter race, we were, yes, believe it or not, only at the seventy five yard mark, it was incredible, I've never seen anything like it in my entire life. The race was over, and naturally Jerry went through to the finals, and me? Well, I was history. At the time, I have to admit I was a little disappointed because I knew I could beat Jerry, but you still have to wish him well. It was the biggest mistake Jerry could have ever had made, he would have to live up to his reputation; he would not only have to come up against the very best runners in the business; but would also, yes, also, be obliged to take random drug test. It was the day of the finals, and again Jerry had won it easily, three months down the line, and he was in another competition. Jerry had won that one too; everyone was ever so pleased for him; all his family and friends and coach's e.t.c they were all ever so pleased for Jerry. Until ten minutes after the race, Jerry was confronted by one of the officials, who insisted on everyone providing a urine sample. Jerry came up positive; there was this big drama!!!!!!!!! And Jerry was banned immediately from the sport; he was also stripped off his gold medal. And made into an entire disgrace. What a waste.......

RAT IN THE KITCHEN

It was my third day of starting my new job at the kitchen; I was warned that there was this "Big Black Rat" called Simon, who terrorized the hell out of staff by just turning up out of the blue, whenever it felt like it, and run riot all over the place, as soon as he got a whiff of the lamb chops which was being roasted in the oven. I was yet to come face to face with the beast, and was rather hoping that I never would have to; but have and behold, around 4.30pm that evening, and we were clearing up for the next morning, when I heard this rustle! I knew it weren't Kate, because she was in the rest room having a cup of tea, and knew whatever it was, it weren't far!!!!!!!! Then in a shear moment of hell, this great big black rat appeared from nowhere; and leapt onto the kitchen table and started knawing its way into the shoulder of lamb, which I left to cool on the table, it was terrifying!!!!! I watched it in horror as it devoured a whole 4 kilo shoulder of lamb, knawing at it like nobody's business, with its 4 inch razor sharp "nasty yellow teeth," he finished it in a matter of seconds. It was terrifying; and in a flash it was gone; it scarpered off like a shot, through the half-open kitchen window, it took of like a blooming maniac. The following morning, I reported it to the environmental health authority, and later that afternoon one of their pest control officers arrived. He was somewhat of a chirpy kind of lad, and assured me that if that dirty rat ever turned up again, it would be in for a shock of his life! I asked him what does he mean by that. He replied well lets just say he'll have more than just the runs to cope with; my interpretation of that was that he was going to give him something to shit himself... Mike the pest control officer had something far more sinister in mind; what he had done, he had carefully mixed some arsenic in a chicken salad, and left it on the kitchen table. The following morning to my horror, lying flat on its side was “Simon.” Out for six he was, the bugger was out cold.

THE BIG RIP OFF

I was fifteen years of age and had just left school. Michael Reynolds my friend reckoned he had a job lined up and that it was somewhat of a good number paying twenty-five nicka a day. That seemed to me at the time a pretty good going rate, if it were true, because the only form of income I was receiving in those days was perhaps a tena a week from the paper round, or perhaps a bit of pocket money maybe a couple of quid a week if I were lucky from my mother when she could afford it. The job we had to do was to gut out an old cellar which looked as though it had been hit by a Luftwaffa bomb, and when we were finished we had to clear the garden that looked like the "tropical rain forest" of Amazonia. The job was huge; and under normal circumstances one would have expected to earn between seventy and eighty pounds a day for all of that garbage, but being just teenagers we were vulnerable and exploited too the max. Anyway, it was the day of work, and having the worse luck in the world it absolutely pelted down that day, and Mr. Morris the man whose house it was managed to convince Michael that he was doing him a favour by allowing him to work in his bloody house. We had to start at eight o'clock sharp, and despite the weather being pissing down with rain, Mr. Morris insisted on us starting off with the garden first. I thought to myself at the time, that's a bit unreasonable? It took us three days to clear out his jungle of a garden. Anyway, we finally got through it. I thought we were going to get paid daily as promised; it wasn't to be, and by the fourth day we had to start on that blitz of a cellar of his; I was laughing at Michael's face, because it was all covered with dust.

It was Friday, and we still hadn't got paid? Mr. Morris was a grumpy old man about sixty years of age who had a squint in his left eye and seemed to me as though he was suffering from alopecia or something, he hardly any hair left on his bald head, and he also walked with a limp. He was a terrible site to look at; but despite his appearance the only thing I was thinking about at the time was when I was going to get paid so I could go out and by myself a new pair of trainers. Three weeks had passed and we were still working away like crazy; we still hadn't got paid, but every Saturday, without fail, Mr. Morris would turn up just to see how his bloody house was getting on; not necessarily to pay us any money, the dirty rat. Anyway, by the fourth week I was at my tethers end with Mr. Morris and confronted the "elusive git" that would only turn up when it pleased him to do so; and do you know what he said to me? He had the audacity to say to me that he's got some more work for me at his other house, and pushed his hands into his dirty pocket and brought out these two scrumfled up old ten pound notes which I interpreted was for a whole weeks worth of work and said to Michael and I eya; one for each of you; the git. He reckoned that he hadn't got paid yet and that he would have the rest in a couple of week's time. Anyway, being upset but at the same time wanting the rest of my money as promised, I didn't want to upset Mr. Morris to the extent that he would just get rid of us and not pay us at all; so we just hung on in there in hope that we would get our full money. The job at the other house was pretty much the same as the last, mainly clearing out. This time we managed to clear his house within a week, but we still hadn't got any more money; and by this time both Michael and I were beginning to scratch our heads saying to each other hold on a minute. Wondering to ourselves whether we were going to get paid at all, because in total we had been working for four weeks, and only had a 30 quid to show for it. Mr. Morris turned up at the end of the week with his limp yelling you finish? Yes Mr. Morris we replied, yes, we're finished, take a look; he took a look, realized that the job had all been done then measly put his hands into his pocket and said eya, revealing two twenty pound notes one for each of us, and walked off with his limp. The bastard.

ROCK BOTTOM

Having lost all my friends, my car, my home, and all the money I had left in the bank. I decided enough was enough! I mean even the cat had lost interest in me, and let me tell you that really did make me feel uncomfortable, she would normally come whizzing up at the door as soon as she heard the gate open, but as soon as she realized that she weren't getting her "Kat Whiskers" anymore, she started giving me the cold shoulder, it was terrible!!!!!! I decided enough was enough! If I was going down, I weren't going down alone! And, I certainly wasn't going to go down without a fight, and that's exactly what I got. It was three o'clock and time for me to sign on, so I set off for my usual fifteen minute walk to the unemployment office, and to my horror, when I got there, the bloody gates were locked, and on the gates, there was a whopping great big banner up saying where on strike! Can you believe it; two minutes later from around the corner came six office workers with signpost's yelling Strike! Strike! Strike! Can you believe it? And worse still, they reckoned, no one gets their benefits until they get their 10% pay rise, promised to them a year ago. Well, as far as I was concerned, that had nothing to do with me, I just wanted my wonga! Now not next year. And to make it worse, have a guess what? There would have to be some four foot nothing ginger head clever dick "midget," come up to me and rub it in, saying we don't get our money, you don't get your money, with his sarcastic look on his "Joe 90" professor looking face. Well, that was enough for me; I told him marvellous en it, making everyone suffer just because you can't get your silly little pay rise. He came up to me in one hell of a rage, saying look mate, its alright for you sitting on your arse all day, but I've got three kids and a wife to support all right. I said to him, well you don't have to take it out on me, and thumped him in the belly, kicked him in the head, and said to him the next time you decide to go on strike, make sure it's for a better reason, like not being able to walk you dick.

RUNNING AWAY

The constant strain of bickering and occasional black eye my mother would end up with, inflicted on from by my dad, was enough to send me on the fast train to London. I couldn't bare to see the family in such turmoil; it was driving me crazy. I was just fifteen for heavens sake; and at the time, I was going through all the changes of puberty, and the usual things that adolescent teenagers go through, and the last thing on my mind was to have to put up with two bickering grown up adults, acting like a bunch of idiots. So I left. I saved up my paper round money, which was around eighty pounds, and took off to London. London was so different from Scarborough, there was all the bright lights etc; back home in Scarborough I had friends, here, it was me myself and I. The first couple of weeks, everything seemed to be so exciting! I only wished I knew someone, because if I had, I'm sure it would have been a lot easier. I had nowhere to stay. However, I was determined to make it by myself; I wasn't going to return back to that "Mad House" because I'm sure, if I did, I'm sure I would have ended up in a "loony bin." So what I did, I found a secluded place where I could kip, and not be disturbed. It was some derelict block of flats, a bit of a tip, but "hey" what do you expect, The Ritz. I thought to myself, if I could just get some work, I'd be all right. I tried everywhere, but no one would employ me, because I had no fixed address. It was terrible. My money was running out rapidly, and I knew I had to do something, because the situation was becoming pretty desperate to say the least. I hadn't a clue what to do, until I met Todd. Todd was seventeen, and came from a similar back ground as myself; the only difference was that, it was Todd who always ended up with the black eyes. Anyway, Todd and I seemed to get on quite well; he seemed to relate to me, especially after I told him of the traumas I had been going through. Todd seemed to empathize with me; he also seemed to be all clued up. He had nothing but sympathy for me. Anyway he said to me, Del, I've got the answer to your prayers; Yes Del, the way I earn my living, I clean car windscreens at traffic lights, it's tough, but you can earn twenty nicka- a- day. Me first day on the road was a bit of a nightmare; all right, I may have earned myself eighteen quid, but I never thought that I would have had to put up with people spitting at me, swearing at me, and trying to run me over, It was terrible. Todd explained to me, that I should take it all with a pinch of salt; he said to me, it's all in the game Del. A month later, I happened to be passing Radio Rentals, and noticed my picture on the television as a missing person; there was also a picture of my mum crying; it really got to me. I had no intention of hurting anybody; how wrong I was; I could see by the looks on my mothers' face, how much in despair she was in, but I was so determined to make it on my own, and be independent. I felt like I had no other option but to get away. After speaking to my mother on the phone and hearing her crying for me to come back home, I explained to her why I resorted to such drastic actions, and explained to her, how I could not handle the situation any longer, and decided to go. She understood; I explained to my mum that the only thing that would make me return home would be if she and dad would stop the arguing. Mum and dad both promised me that they would, and things did gradually get better.

WHY YOU DIRTY RAT

Thirty-three years I'd been working at the damn law firm and just because I was approaching middle age the bosses had conspired against me and were planning something sinister. William and Jenny had been planning for months on how and when they were going to bring my contract to an abrupt end, and bring in new blood. We had a pretty good relationship up until then; but recently I began noticing subtle hint's, like, oh Tom, wouldn't you just like to win the lottery so that you can have an early retirement? Wouldn't we all I thought to myself. I liked working; it gave something to do. It was Christmas Eve, and we were all together at the Christmas party when William introduced me to a new employee he was employing in the new year, because he thought I needed a hand in the post room?? Hand in the post room; I had over thirty years experience working in the post room and was quite competent thank you very much William; I am perfectly fine thank you, I said in my mind. He knew I could manage ok and that I really didn't need any assistance, but William knew exactly what he was doing? He was gradually easing me out gently…. I left the Christmas party thinking to myself, the dirty rat was only secretly planning to get rid of me, and give me a pat on the back and say thank you very much you boring old fart ….goodbye; that's what he was thinking? That's what he was thinking. Six weeks into the New Year and I was called up to William's office; I knocked on the door, knock knock, (come in Tom); William answered; I walked in, and Jenny was standing by his side with a pretty glum look on her face; I wondered to myself, what's the matter with her, why is she looking so glum. Anyway, Tom started talking to me and said in these very words, now Tom, I know your coming up to retirement soon, yes…… I replied, and I know that your back has been playing up recently, no, I thought to myself?

So, we've decided that it would be in your best interest if you were to hang up your boots now and have an early retirement; what a bloody cheek I thought to myself. My back is all right now I replied. (William) no… Tom lets not get into an argument about this. There's also going to be a lot of heavy lifting going on in the near future, and we think that Pete is the fitter man for the job. So what we'll do, we'll pay you for up until the end of the month, then you must leave. I walked off with my head down thinking to myself, how could you do this to me, how could you do this to me, and just as I was about to shut the door, I heard them giggling; hee hee hee. I thought to myself, why you dirty rat.

I'LL SEE YOU IN COURT

This is a story about a bitter feud between two members of a family; Mick and Sue. The argument was over the ownership of the house, Sam; their father had left them when he died. Three months after Sam's death, rage broke out; I got a rollicking of a phone call from Mick saying that he wants to put the deeds in his name; Mick's reason for this was that I already had a council place of my own which I share with my husband Tom. What a cheek I thought to myself; Alright, I've got a council place of my own but it's shared, and if, I'm not saying it's going to happen, but let's say Tom decided he was leaving me, well, I would be out on my ear, and I certainly weren't going to allow that to happen. I tried explaining this to Mick, but he was so pig head ignorant, he wouldn't listen to a word I had to say. Just because he was the eldest, he thought he had all the rights. Things started to get out of hand when Mick announced that he was getting married to Mary. Don't get me wrong, I was happy for him; but my main concern was what were the implications of this marriage likely to be? I thought to myself, what might be the result of this arrangement; it could leave me without any say? My primary concern was that, what rightfully belonged to me, what I was entitled too, I should certainly have. Anyway, I couldn't keep what I had inside of me any longer, so I went around to the house. Mick opened the door, and the look on his face, wasn't exactly a welcoming look; the look was one of that he weren't exactly pleased see me, and he hardly seemed as though he wanted to let me in the place where I actually grew up, and lived for the past twenty odd years until I met Tom. I mean the place where I grew up suddenly gave me the feeling of hostility; a feeling that I never had before, it was terrible….

Anyway, I squeezed past Mick, and before I could utter a blinking word, Mick stopped me dead in my traps and said, now look Susan! Don't waste your breath, the house belongs to me, and that's the end of it. I'm the eldest, dad left it to me, and that's the end of the story. Well, I weren't having any of it. I said to Mick you got no right! Right, he said, I've got all the right; and before I could say another word, guess who had to butt her big mouth into it? His wife Mary. I was so stunned, because this was a private matter; and guess what she said to me? She said, Sue, you've got a place of your own, why don't you just leave us alone. I was so upset; I told her, why don't you mind your f..........own business, and slammed the door and walked out. I was so upset by the way the two of them had ganged up on me like that; I mean, there were only two of us in our family, Mick and I, and although dad did not write a will, he would have been absolutely turning over in his grave to hear how to two of us were squabbling over the house like this. Three months down the line, and I hadn't heard a word from Mick, so, I decided to give him a ring to see whether the matter could be settled amicably; and to my horror Sue picked up the phone, and I heard her say to Mick, its that sister of yours again; and as soon as Mick came to the phone, believe it or not his first words were, what do you want now? I told him, I'll see you in court.

I'LL SHOW YOU MINE, IF YOU'LL SHOW ME YOUR'S

I've always wondered why Mary had decided to keep it away from me; after all, we had known each other for years; I know we were not boyfriend girlfriend sort of thing, but we shared a lot in common; we were both into arts and crafts and had met at college, and remained good friends ever since. We would go to the museums, galleries and craft fairs together and have such fun times together. I could sense that Mary wasn't her usual self when Mary started to become a little aloof and distant towards me. She would do her utmost best to avoid me; and would always be out when I knocked at her home. This type of behaviour pattern was extremely unusual for Mary, because she was quite a homely type person and a bit of a loner really, and usually, if she wasn't in my company or at her mother's who only lived across the road, you could count on it that Mary would be at her flat. Anyway, what had happened was, Mary had secretly found herself a boyfriend, and did not want me to know; I think she must have been scared perhaps of ruining our platonic relationship. But I also think that deep down, Mary secretly fancied me, but did not know how to tell me; I can't say for sure, but I'm sort of convinced that that was the case. Anyway, she was sure as hell was acting pretty strange about it. I enjoyed Mary's company and loved being around her; I wouldn't have wanted anything to change that, even if she had found herself a boyfriend. Anyway, one afternoon this mystery boyfriend of her's eventually came out from out of the wood works; he was "Tommy Fisher" this short geezer with spots all over his face, who wore baggy trousers and was in our class at college. Tommy always sat at the back of the class, and would always shout for attention, saying sir, can you repeat that please. I think he had a hearing problem or something. Anyway, it was he that Mary was

secretly seeing and wanted to keep it under wraps. I couldn't quite work out why Mary was so scared of coming out into the open about it, and just tell me that she'd found herself a boyfriend. But have and behold, Mary wanted to keep it a secret; but sooner or later, it had to come out, because you can run but you can't hide. The Funny thing about it was, I think the real reason why Mary went out with Tommy was to see whether I would get jealous; she didn't really want Tommy Fisher, the "Looser;" she only found him to see how I would react; she really wanted me, but because I never asked her out quickly enough, main reason is because I did not want to spoil our special relationship. She did a dirty one on me. I guess, deep down, all I wanted from Mary was to declare her feelings towards me; that's all, nothing more, and nothing less.
I hadn't been totally honest with Mary either, because I had done something Mary had no idea of too. Because, without telling her, secretly, I went and had a tattoo with a love heart saying, Mary 4 Derek. I guess, deep down, I too was just as scared to declare my feelings towards her, and did not have the courage, so I kept them suppressed, in hope that one day Mary would reveal herself to me. When I found out that Mary was seeing that rat, I too began to distant myself from her; I did this only to give her a little space with her "new fella." But after about five weeks of not seeing Mary, Mary had missed me, and could not understand why I had been distancing myself from her. I told her the real reason why, and to my delight, she split from Tommy. Mary just couldn't live with the fact that it was I she really wanted; I said to her me? Yes, you Derek, I've always fancied you, but did not know how to say it; and had only went out with Tommy to see how you would react. I also have a confession to make Mary, I said to Mary; I have felt the same way ever since we first met, and to prove it, look, look what I had done. I lifted up my Tee Shirt, revealing my tattoo, which read "Derek 4 Mary."

Mary laughed!!!!! What you laughing for Mary I said; it was then that Mary lifted up her blouse revealing her tattoo above her navel, saying Mary and Derek forever. Having seen that, I just fell into her arms totally overwhelmed and besotted with what I had seen.

HE'S IN MY SPACE

My wife Sue and I had recently moved to the suburbs after finally having enough of urban living. I was ever so pleased with the house we had bought. It had everything, its own private drive, and swimming pool; and the price we paid for it, it was just under £250,000, a price you would find difficult getting a decent flat, let alone a five bedroom house with all the trimmings. After all the pain of moving all our bits and pieces in, I thought to myself, we can finally put our feet up and settle down with some peace and quiet, without the constant pain of hearing the siren's of police - ambulance - and fire engine's going off every five minutes. Well, there was no police cars or ambulances or fire engines going off, but there was this nuisance of a car, constantly blocking my drive, and I would always have to squeeze past it; things really got to me when I noticed a scratch to the body of my car; I knew I didn't do it, because I'd have realized it. I thought perhaps it might have been Sue who clipped it on her way in, and hadn't realized; perhaps she did it on the way back from shopping or something. I asked Sue whether it was her who did it, and she vehemently denied that she had anything to do with it; and I believed her. I reckoned to her it's got to be the owners of that bloody car en it; I asked her if she knew who it belonged too, and she replied, no darling, I can't say I do. Damn cheek I replied. It was a Saturday morning, and Sue was off on her usual shopping trip; and once again, that bloody green car was sitting blocking the drive, and Sue had to squeeze past it again; only, this time she ended up braking the wing mirror off, and to make it worse, when she had returned, all his mates had turned up with their cars, leaving Sue having to park a quarter of a mile down the road, and having to walk all the way back with all those shopping bags. When I heard of this I was furious!! I wanted to find out who it was who actually owned the bloody car, but most importantly, who it was who had the bloody cheek to vacate my space; so I knocked on either side of my neighbours doors; I knew it could not have been the one on the right, because she was an elderly woman who lived alone, but I thought she might however point me in the right direction towards the culprit it did belong too; it was the neighbour who lived on the left, they had a son, who had a friend, who would visit almost every day, and park his retched old banger car in my space. Anyway, I knocked the door, and out came running a little boy, I think he must have been about five or something. I asked him, is his father there? Yes he replied, daddy daddy, there's someone to see you; the boy's father replied from the kitchen area of his house who just happened to be doing a spot of cooking; tell him I'm coming he yelled; he came to the door a few seconds later; it was the first time we were to meet, and it could not have been under any worse circumstances. Anyway, I explained to him how the green car was blocking my drive, he replied, it doesn't belong to me; and shouted from the bottom of the stairs to his son's friend "Jerry"!!!!!!! You're blocking the next door neighbours drive; Jerry reluctantly replied.... I'm coming, I could hear from the bottom of the stairs, that some sort of computer game or something was going on, and it would appear that Jerry was so into his game, that he did not want to be distracted. I later found out that my neighbours name was Frank, and he could see that Jerry was taking his time; and he also wanted to get back to what he was doing, so he took about three steps up the stairs and called again, Jerry!!!!!! This time he did come out, and when he got to my drive, he took a look at the situation of where he had parked his car, and had the temerity to tell me, you can get a tank through that! What you on about! I was furious!!!!!!!!!!!! He did move his car, after at least ten minutes of negotiation, and I told him that I would appreciate it if he wouldn't park it there in the future. A week later, I was returning from work, and noticed that same bloody green car again on my drive; I jumped out of my car, dashed over to Frank's house, this time believe it or not, the culprit Jerry answered the door, I grabbed him by the throat, and told him to move that bloody banger away from my door now!!! Now I said!!! He was terrified. The following day, I noticed my beautiful sunflower that was slightly towering the dividing hedge had been chopped off, and was lying on the earth. I asked Sue did she cut the heads off the sunflower. No she replied, no, I didn't do it, I knew it could be only one person.

THE STALKER

I had just moved to the suburbs after having decided on getting away from the hustle and bustle of urban living. The main reasons I guess for leaving was because of the ever increasing excessive fume levels; it would often leave me feeling fatigued queezy and tired, and being a single woman without any children I thought to myself I can go anywhere I liked, and I did. I found a beautiful little flat within days of looking, and I was so pleased with myself. It was exactly what I was looking for; it was a beautiful little flat above a newsagent; just right I thought to myself, just right. I got settled in and settled down to my normal routine, and started doing the things I would normally do back in London, like waking up at six and going for a quick jog around the green which was literally just a stone throw across the road. That would be enough to give me the kick start I needed for the day. It put me in the mood to face the day and also it cleared my lungs which of course if I hadn't, they would have felt like a vacuum cleaner from all the fumes caught from urban living. I felt so much fresher after doing my jog. The air was ever so much cleaner here; it was lovely. On the way back from my run I would usually get a newspaper from the shop downstairs. I don't know but after about three weeks of living here, do you ever get that feeling that someone is watching you? Well, that's exactly how I felt. I was right. After about five weeks I got a letter in the post from a secret admirer saying that he's been watching me for weeks, and that he was totally besotted with me, and how he wanted to marry me!!!!! I was absolutely shocked; I had no idea of whom it might be; and I was rather hoping that it would be some kind of practical joke and fade away, it wasn't to be. Anyway, after having received some thirty-two letters, sometimes four to five times a week, I decided enough was enough I wanted to find out who it was and called my brother Derek and told him about what was happening to me. I wasn't quite sure whether or not to call Derek, because Derek had such an awful temper on him. He once broke a guy's neck in the pub just for putting his arms around me. Derek thought he was taking advantage of his baby sister, and wasn't havingany of it. For all I knew this man who was stalking me might have been genuine; but I wasn't going to take any chances. So, Derek came down and stayed with me for a bit. The letters still came flooding in, and Derek asked me again and again are you sure you don't know who's responsible for doing this? Each time I replied I have no idea Derek. I don't know what it was but Derek had a hunch that it might have been the elderly owner of the newsagents downstairs; and asked me, what about "im" downstairs? No… I said, he wouldn't do a thing like that. So, what Derek did was he parked his car across the road, and when it was around 5 'o clock, he hid in his car. I went off for my usual run at six, and just as I left, Derek noticed Mr. James the dirty old newsagent step out of his shop and sneak upstairs to my flat to place yet another letter through my letterbox. But this time he was about to be "Collard" because just as Mr. James was about to put his unwanted letter through my letter box Derek grabbed him by the neck!!!!!!!!!!!! Mr. James turned around in terror!! Derek said to him; hold it mate and took the letter off him and ripped it open only to find out that he was right all along. It was that dirty old man Mr. James who was making his sisters life such a misery. By this time I was just returning back from my jog, only to find Mr. James held in one of Derek's firm headlock, and belting him around the face repeatedly; I shouted stop! Derek, you'll kill him. Derek seemed as though he wanted to kill him; but I finally broke him off. Mr. James's face looked like it had hit a Double Decker bus. Derek wanted to finish him off there and then. After Derek had finished with him, Derek said, I'm going to bring him down to the station. We brought Mr. James down to the police station, and still in Derek's firm grip; and as soon as Mr. James spotted the police officer, he quickly claimed that Derek had done him in, and to my horror they arrested Derek, and done him for assault. They cautioned Mr. James, and let him go. I thought to myself that's bloody justice for you.

SUCCESS

This is a story about an intelligent black man called (Joe), with a Masters Degree in economics, who gets a job as a Stock Brokers in the city. But the society he finds himself working in is predominately white and upper class. Joe tried everything he could to be accepted, he even goes off to University to learn foreign languages, and he completes his course and is fluent in speaking four foreign languages, French, German, Spanish, and Italian. He even buys himself a pair of glasses so that he would appear, or least give the impression, that he really is intelligent. He even tries to hang out with his colleagues at social gaverings, like places like the local pub and dinner parties; he works his way right up to the very top of the his profession, only to realize that one of the chairmen will not accept him as one of the board of directors. Realizing that all Joe is really allowed to do, is all the shoveling work, Joe ends up in one hell of swearing match with (Jim), one of the directors who will not accept him. The confrontation Joe has with Jim takes place whilst they're in the lift together. Joe said to Jim I know why you won't accept me as one of the board of directors, I know? It's because I'm black isn't it? Go on, just tell me the truth? Jim say's yeah that's bloody right, we don't want any of your lot on the bloody board. Jim was rejected several times before he himself was accepted on the board; reason being, was that Jim had poor communication skills, this was mainly because he would stutter constantly, and because he refused to be bilingual, a skill which was really essential for his position, because a lot of the firms business was done overseas. This made Jim extremely envious of Joe in having those vital language skills. Well, what had happened was Joe called Jim just about every name under the sun whilst they were in the lift together, and when they finally reached the 24th floor,

Jim's face had turned as red as a beetroot, from the shock of his ordeal with Joe. Jim was so upset by his ordeal, he orders a security guard to throw Joe out of the building, immediately!!! He calls security, and three of them come along, grabs Joe by the scruff of his neck, and throws him out onto the street; Jim follows, writes a cheque, and throws the cheque at Joe yelling out, you're sacked!!!!!!!!!!!! Joe decides to get revenge! He felt so embarrassed by people watching him being booted out onto the streets like that, he say's to himself, no way man, I'm not going to let him get away with this, and decides to get revenge, first of all by letting down all four of Jim's tyres, then, smashing Jim's windows of his car; Joe not only does this to Jim's car, but he also does this to the cars of all the other directors of the company; it wasn't long before all four of them were telling each other of their experiences. Suddenly it came to the attention of (Burt), one of the senior director on the board, who say's to Jim, you know that kid you had thrown out onto the streets the other day, Oh.... what's his name? Joe, that's right, Joe; it could well be him you know Jim, (Burt) he's not a bad little worker you know Jim? I think you kind of handled him a little rough Jim? What do you say Jim? .... Yeah, I guess I did. What do you say Jim, we give him a chance? (Jim) ....Yeah all right then. Burt phones Joe up and arranges a meeting down the pub. Joe was not expecting Jim to be there, but Jim comes over to Joe and apologizes for his behaviour. Joe's is reinstated; and in the first year Joe turns the company's profits over by a whopping 50%, and at the same time opens the door for other black graduates like his-self. Jim was not only resentful to Joe because he was black, he was envious that Joe had better communication skills than what he had, and hated the fact that he could be more important to the company than he him self. Jim had been rejected several times before he was finally accepted in a senior position, and he thought to himself ere comes this young black man half his age thinking he owns the joint! Jim was fortunate enough to be accepted onto the board, not necessarily for any skills that Jim possessed, but the fact that he had saved Burt from having a serious accident of nearly losing his fingers on the guillotine machine, when Jim grabbed held hold of the lever preventing it from causing Burt a nasty injury. Burt felt as though he owed Jim a favour, and promoted him on the board. And from that moment on, Burt and Jim had become quite close friends. As time went on at the firm, Jim began to accept Joe a little more, after realizing just how hard Joe had to study to get to where he is today.

TAXI

It was the 24th of December and it was Christmas Eve, and the girls had arranged to go out partying at Chino's night-spot. There were five of us in total, Jane, Carla, Pam, Theresa, and myself. We got to the night-club and was having such a nice time; it was so funny because there happened to be a fancy dress party going on at the time, and neither of had a clue that anything of this activity was going to be happening, so we just turned up as normal. Anyway, there was this man who was dressed in a gorilla suit, who started chasing after me, he scared the life out of me; and when he finally caught me, he took hold of my hands, and started doing the waltz with me, it was so funny. By this time, the rest of the girls were all a bit tipsy, so I knew they were having a good time. The time was around 3.30am and the night was narrowing to an end, and being that we all lived relatively close to one and other, not more than a few miles apart or so, so we all jumped in the same cab.

It worked out in a way that I was last to be dropped off, and by this time I was feeling a little bit tired, well, to be frank with you, all I wanted to do was to go to sleep; the driver on the other hand didn't seem to mind, as he must of been saying to himself, I'm going to make a packet tonight? Anyway, after having dropped the rest of the girls off, there was just Pam and I who were left in the cab. Anyway, I decided to drop Pam off first because she only lived two blocks away from where I lived, and was more or less on route to her address, and then I would get dropped off last, leaving me alone in the cab. Anyway, after I dropped Pam off, I told the driver just carry on straight down the road then turn left at the lights; we got to the lights and the bloody driver kept going straight on!!!!!!!!!! I shouted you've missed it! You missed the turning! Then suddenly I heard a click on the door! He had locked it from the inside, I shouted at him turn around! He just ignored me…….

DOUBLE TROUBLE

This is a story about a organized counterfeit group of money swindlers who start off distributing their fake money down local market places, buying small item's for under a tena with a fifty pound note and receiving forty odd pounds in change; they also decide to use the money to get into nightclubs and really live it up, buying bottles of champagne and brandy, and also buying cars from dealers and selling it the very next day for trade price. They have no partiality for ordinary people either, because they also buy cars via the local papers, from people wishing to sell their cars. They even had the audacity to book their selves a holiday in the Canary Islands; I mean these guys were really living it up to the max. One day the gang of four went one step too far when they decided to get smashed out of their heads and buy a kilo of cocaine from some big time drug dealer called Boris. they do the deal and think every thing is as sweet as a nut, until Boris goes to put the dodgy notes into his bank account and not realizing that he is about to deposit counterfeit money into his bank account he hands over the money to the cashier, the cashiers holds the money up in the air. The drug dealer replies, they're as good as gold; she secretly presses the automatic security lock to lock the doors. This switch simultaneously alerts the police station; the police arrive in a matter of seconds, as they just happened to be around the corner in their police car doing their usual patrol. They arrived and arrested "Boris." Boris puts up a struggle, but it's no use, because there are three police officers, and all the bank staff against one man. Boris is arrested and brought down to the police station, he's searched, and a small amount of cocaine is found on him; they also find a flick knife in his pocket. They caution him and charged him. Meanwhile, Boris is

being detained at the police station; his home is being tipped upside down by the police, who are ever so eager and determined to find more drugs or money. Luckily for Boris his shipment of cocaine which was just bought in had just been placed by his brother Steve, to a customer.
His brother Steve had sold five kilos on his behalf just moments after he had left for the bank, and there was nothing left in the house. Back at the police station, Boris is charge on three counts of having in his possession one thousand pounds worth of counterfeit notes, ten milligrams of cocaine, and also an offensive weapon, namely a flick knife. Boris is charged, and due to appear at Snaresbrook crown court in a month. Boris already has a string of convictions and is furious about the guy's who done him a bum deal. He keeps on muttering to himself in rage, I'm going to kill those guys. Meanwhile Boris is out on bail and determined as hell to get those guy's, so he gets together with his brothers, they tool themselves up and set out on the search for the four dildos's who stitched him up. They search everywhere, they search the clubs, the pubs, the casino's, everywhere, to no avail, until one day, three weeks later, Steve, Boris's brother spots one of the guy's with his girlfriend going into a house just a few blocks away from where they had done the deal. Steve gets on the mobile straight away, and within minutes, two cars full of Steve's heavy and hard looking underworld mates arrive all tooled up with gun's, baseball bats, knifes the lot; all concealed in their jackets. They pull outside the house, knock the door, the girlfriend answers the door, they brush her aside, rampage the house, finds "Micky," one of the gang members who done the dud deal with Boris, beats the hell out of him with their baseball bat, and tells him they know what he did, and demanded the kilo of cocaine back. Micky cries out……., my brother has got it. They escort him and his girlfriend to where Micky's brother is, down the local pub, shows him the pistol, proving that they mean business. They arrive at the pub where Colin Micky's

brother is drinking; spots him playing a game of pool; they drag him out by the scuff of his neck, and demand him to lead them to where their cocaine is. Boris explains what had happened to him, and what kind of sentence he is looking at, and demands that they come up with thirty grand by the end of the week to secure him, just in case anything happens to him, and he goes to jail. And the arrangement is that they keep the girl for security. Boris explains that she'll be released on delivery of the money, and Boris says to Micky this time those notes, they better be good ones. Steve realizes he has some hard work to do. Anyway, they get to work straight away, not coming home for three days. They were out there none stop trying to get the money together, and they just about made it on time, and on the day before Boris is due to appear in court. They release the girl, and that's the end of the saga for now. Boris goes to court and receives a heavy fine of four thousand pounds, and fifty-two hours community service, helping the elderly people; he was lucky to get away with not going to jail.

THE HORNY VICAR

I knew he fancied me by the way he kept smiling at me when he gave me the body of Christ. It wasn't long before he was announcing that if anyone would like to speak to him about any personal matter's they should come along at 6.30pm, and meet him in the confession box. I left it for around six weeks, but I knew I had to get what was on my mind, off my mind. What it was, it was one of the quire boy's I had fancied for months; I wasn't even sure whether he knew, but I just needed someone to talk to about it, and I thought to myself surely the priest should be someone who I could confide in, and get advise from. Because I did not want to live in sin. So I decided that I would go and see him that evening. I arrived a bit early so that's I could be the first to be seen; and when I got there, I went into the confession room and spoke to him from the other side of the wall. It was a little disconcerting at first but I had to get it off my chest; so I told him, and once I got it off my chest, I felt much better. Father assured me that it was normal to have these thoughts; he said to me that these feeling's are only human feelings and I've nothing to worry about he said. I was so pleased with his answer.

After he had told me this he asked me to come around the back so that he could bless my body!!!!! I replied rather naively; oh thank you very much father; if I'd only known just what that horny bugger had on his mind, I'd have never had gone. Anyway, I went around the back only to be greeted with a kiss on the mouth; I thought to myself this is a little unusual for a vicar? Then he held my hand and led me up the altar. He told me to hold my hands out so that he could wash them with holy water. Then he started to rub my breast!!!!!! I said no!!!!!! And ran off, he then gave chase, chasing me around the altar like some lyntho maniac. I screamed! This is not right; he just kept on chasing after me. I said to him leave me alone, and screamed, and ran off in the direction of the main door. And when I got out of the church, I said to him I never want to see you again, you horrible man you….

I WANT HIM

This is a story about a girl twin who decides to run off with her sisters' boyfriend, after finding her sister in bed with another man; Jane was absolutely livid with her sister Sarah for doing that to Roy, because in the beginning Jane originally had a crush on Roy; but Roy had chosen Sarah because she had approached him first, much to Jane's disappointment. The couple first met at their work's Christmas party, when Roy got a little tipsy and Sarah offered Roy a lift home. Jane would often go on dates together with Roy and Sarah; they were very close, and were seldom apart from one and other. Roy on the other hand didn't seem to mind at all; or if he did, he didn't say anything. There were times, when we would go to the cinema, and Roy would be sitting in the middle of us cuddling us both; and passers by would often have difficulty telling which one of us he was actually seeing. Jane would often get aroused by Roy's cuddles, but knew she couldn't possibly take it any further, but deep down envied Sarah for having such luck; nevertheless she remained loyal to her sister for family sake. Until one afternoon, whilst the both of us were at work together, Sarah told me that she wasn't feeling well; it was a cover up; she wanted to go home and have a whale of a time with Jim our boss. Roy was ever so kind to Sarah, and I can't understand why Sarah would do such a horrible thing to him. I was so bitter when I left work fifteen minutes early, only to find the two of them stark naked on the kitchen floor. I was so shocked; I just slammed the door and ran across the road over to Roy's house. Fortunately enough he happened to be in. Roy would sometimes found it difficult in telling the difference between the two of us, and because

I had witnessed my sister doing such a horrible thing to this sweet man, I just pretended that I was Sarah.

The next day, Sarah had the cheek to play lovey couples with Roy, pretending that nothing had happened. Well, she wasn't kidding me; I had seen her with my bare two eyes. Sarah was so cold; she seems to thrive on playing Russian roulette; despite the fact that Roy only lived across the road; it's almost as if she wanted to be caught by him. Knowing Sarah, she probably would have got a kick out of seeing two grown up men squabbling over her. I'm sure she would have loved it; well, I wasn't going to sit down and see a dear friend get hurt like that. To me, it just wasn't fair. So the following day I waited for Roy to come around that evening, as he usually did, prompt on 6 'o clock, and I confronted Sarah in the living room about it. I knew Roy would be devastated, but I just couldn't hold it in, I had to get it out and off my mind. I was right, Roy was devastated; after I had told him what Sarah had done. He just held his hands to his face and burrowed himself to tears; I was so sorry for him, the poor fella, Sarah had hurt him so badly. My intention wasn't to split them up; I just wanted Roy to know that the sweet little darling sister of mine wasn't the goody two shoes that she portrays to be. After I said what I had to say, I left, and went up to my bedroom, leaving the two of them to settle their differences. I could hear from my bedroom one hell of an argument!!! I rushed down the stairs, only to find my mother, who had just arrived in from work trying to rip the two of them apart. Roy wanted to kill Sarah; Sarah was lucky mother was there to stop it; mother said to Roy, I think you should leave! I couldn't bare to stay in the same house as Sarah, so I left and went over to Roy's. I knocked on Roy's door and said him it's me Sarah, pretending to be her; he opened the door and let me in; he poured me a glass of scotch; and after about a hour and three servings of scotch whisky, I guess the drink had taken its toll on us both, and there was only one thing left to do, the bedroom.

I DO

Mother was right; I knew I was doing the wrong thing when James asked me to married him at the registry office. I wanted a church wedding with all the family and friends present; but James wanted a quiet old wedding. He said the money would be better off spent on furniture for the house; he had a point; but this was my special day; we didn't even have a honeymoon. James just carted me off to the local boozer. I stayed there for a couple of hours, but I couldn't take it any longer with all the smoke etc, so I left and went home. I don't even think James had noticed me leaving; he seemed more into his game of snooker than anything else; it was terrible. He got home that evening stinking of beer and cigarette's; and shouted from the top of the hall; Barbara make us a cup of black coffee will you luv; I replied why did you stay out so late James? We've only just got married and I wanted you here with me, not down the blasted pub. Don't you start he replied in a dreary tone of voice; I'm not in the mood or right.... And he just slumped his self down on the sofa. I made him the coffee he asked for; and watched him go into a trance as he watched American Football on sky TV. He hardly seemed as though he wanted to come to bed with me that night; I called him several times, trying to temp him to come up stairs into bed; he replied, not now Barbara; can't you see I'm watching the footy! Go to bed and I'll join you as soon as it's finished he said. The time was fast approaching 3.30am, and still no sign of James; so I decided I'd go downstairs to see just what had happened to him; I walked down the stairs into the lounge, only to find James spread out on the sofa snoring his head off. I was gutted and just walked up the stairs wishing that I should have never of

married him. Three months later and things still hadn't improved; he still weren't giving me the attention I wanted; and was still coming home late from the pub; it was hardly the married life I had planned. Then, one day, this rather attractive salesman came and knocked at the door, trying to sell me a new kitchen unit. Our home was in need of a new unit, but that wasn't my top priority. But he was……….
Anyway, we started having an affair; Stewart gave me all the attention I needed; much more than I was receiving from my husband; but I respected my marriage vows, meaning marriage was for life.
One afternoon James came home early from work, totally out of the blue, and Stewart was there; with only his boxer short's on; oh my god, oh my god I panicked, as James called from the bottom of the stairs; Barbara; there's a meeting on at work and they've given us the afternoon off; and before I could say Jack Robinson, he had rushed up the stairs, only to find to his dismay Stewart; what's the bloody hells'going on ere? James indignantly asks, as he looks on at Barbara with great consternation, I wanna know, what the bloody hells going on ere? James asks again; Barbara tries to explain, only to receive one hell of a slap from James; eeeh, heeeeeeee Barbara cries; Stewart responds, I think I'd better be going; James replies damn right you had better be going; and if I ever see you here again, I'll break your bloody neck alright. James asks Barbara, why she had cheated on him? Barbara replies to James, you just weren't giving me any attention James; and I felt lonely; I needed to be loved, and you just didn't seem to be interested. (James), why don't we go away; just the two of us; we need to put the spark back into our marriage; or it's just not going to work; what do you say Barbara? Yeah all right, all right, we'll go away, and put things right. (James), I love you Barbara and I want it to work; (Barbara) so do I. James; they went away and gradually things started to get better.

THE BARKING DOG

Woof Woof, Woof Woof, Woof Woof. Shit! It's at it again; it's getting on my bloody nerves! If that C..... Don't put a quietner on that dog of ease, I'm going to feed it some poison; I've been down the council, they can't be bothered, I've tried speaking to the owner, he won't admit there's a problem, what's it gonna take ay?

Woof Woof, Woof Woof, Woof Woof. Shit! I've had it, I'm going down to that bloody owner again, and I'm going to give him a peace of my mind; and as soon as I knocked on his door, out came running that ruddy mongrel of he's trying to bite my foot!! It's all right he reckons, he won't bite? That retched thing of he's was half chewing off my feet. Get back boy he reckons; the dog seemed reluctant in doing so; (Mr. James) get back… Look Mr. James, I don't mean to be a pest, but I'm finding it extremely hard in concentrating; it's nothing personal, but with your dog barking all day like that, it's driving me up the wall. The dog seemed to understand what I was talking about and seemed to me as if he was getting angrier!! Yeah, all right he says reluctantly, I'll put him inside. Three hours later, he put him back outside again! Woof Woof, Woof Woof, Woof Woof, Woof Woof, Woof Woof! That's it, I've had it; I fly down the stairs, not bothering to wait for the lift because it was to slow, and the anger I had inside of me just couldn't hold; my patience had worn thin; I banged on the door, Mr. James he sees me in a rage, and would you believe it, he set's his dog onto me; get him boy he reckons; the dog came running after me like some raving lunatic; I did a quick u turn and scarpered down the street! Spotting a lamppost, I climbed up it quickly before that maniac dog of his had a chance to sink his horrible filthy green teeth into me. It stood at the bottom of the lamp- post growling, wishing I would come down so that it could eat me up. Mr. James came walking casually down the road; I screamed get that retched dog away from me!! “Butch” he reckons, come on boy; grabbing it by the collar, he laughs; and says, he won’t bother us again.

THE HUNT FOR THE BLACK PANTHER

Rumours had it that several spottings had been made about a large black cat lurking around the country side; and the thought of an attack had been terrifying the locals for months; we had three small children all under the age of seven and was extremely concerned about their safety. The council had made some steps towards tracing this elusive cat, but after about four weeks without any trace or sight of it, it would appear as though they had given up. Until one afternoon a local farmer called Joe had noticed that one of his sheep was missing. So Joe decided to go out and look for his lost sheep; and it wasn't long before Joe found his sheep's head lying beside a tree. Joe was furious because business was bad as it was. Joe had a hunch that this type of attack could only have been carried out by a large cat or dog; and having heard the rumours about the sighting of a large cat, Joe's suspicion alerted him to think that yes, this cat must be the culprit. Joe was only too eager to catch his enemy. So Joe took his rifle and his knife and set off on the hunt for the Black Panther. Joe was away for three days determined as hell to find this cat, sleeping out rough in the forest. It wasn't long before Joe was to meet face to face with his arch enemy; the time was approximately three o'clock in the morning, and crouched down beside a small pond, Joe spotted the beast licking his lips; it seemed as though he was cleaning off blood from its mouth from an earlier kill. So quietly Joe crept up at it and aimed his rifle and shot at it, bang! But Joe missed it, and the cat ran away. Joe quickly loaded his riffle up for a second shot but could not do so quickly enough, and in an instant the Panther had appeared from nowhere and leaped onto Joe's neck and bit him killing him instantly. Joe's body was found a day later and a full scale hunt was on for the Black Panther. I was absolutely devastated when I heard what had happened to Joe. This killing had got me worried as hell; thinking to my self it could be me or my children next. Joe was a good friend to the locals in the village; Kate and I did not know him personally because we had just moved to the village. We decided to move to the country to get away from the hustle and bustle of urban living to settle down to somewhere peaceful and quiet; we thought to our selves that it would be better for the kids, only to be put on a full scale alert of this nightmare of a beast lurking around and ready to pounce on some poor person. Well it wasn't going to get me or my family. I had something planned for the brute. So I got together my automatic pistol, my flame torch, a net and a dagger, and set off on the hunt. After about a mile of walking deep into the countryside I spotted footprints leading towards a cave, so I followed the prints and tentatively entered into the cave; the cave didn't appeared to be that deep and I had a strong suspicion that it was in there. So I gavered together some hay and decided that it was better for me to smoke him out because it was quite dark in there and difficult for me to see. So I made a fire out of the hay and placed it in about twenty yards or so into the cave. It wasn't long before the beast came running out… and just as it emerged from the cave looking somewhat disorientated I shot it in the head three times, I killed it instantly, it was dead, and dragged it back to the village, and told everyone…. It was a much awaited sigh of relief to the locals to finally be at peace and not be this type of alert.

Printed in Great Britain
by Amazon

69672970R00102